The Mark Fam.

Thomas Skyler
Foothills Preacher

Please return To ↑ Route 2, Box 959
Catlett, Va.
by 22019
Ralph Connor

Edited by Michael Phillips
for the Sunrise *Stories of Yesteryear* series

SUNRISE BOOKS
PUBLISHERS
EUREKA, CALIFORNIA 95501
A Division of One Way, Ltd.

Originally published as *The Sky Pilot* in 1899 by The Westminster Company, Limited, Toronto, Canada.

This edited edition, *Thomas Skyler: Foothills Preacher*, Copyright © 1988 by Sunrise Books, Publishers as Volume 2 in the Sunrise "Stories of Yesteryear" Series.

Printed in the United States of America.

Library of Congress Catalog Card Number
87-82629

ISBN 0-940652-07-2

DEDICATION

This Sunrise edition of *The Sky Pilot* is dedicated to the memory of the man whose visionary enthusiasm for the writings of Ralph Connor provided the inspired goad toward their republication, Harold B. Frazee, who went home to be with his Lord during the completion of this project.

THE SUNRISE STORIES
OF YESTERYEAR

Stories of Yesteryear is a series of novels which hearkens back to nostalgic times of bygone years —times which, if not easier, somehow yet seem less complex, even with their hardships, than these present frenzied years of the late 20th century. The series includes old publications which have been lost to the present day reading public, but which in their own day were best-sellers. Most of these have been edited for Sunrise and brought back into print in updated format so that you may today enjoy quality, wholesome fiction through great works and classics of the past. In addition the series will occasionally offer new stories about historical times and places of past generations. All the books in the *Stories of Yesteryear* series are stories about people with real joys and problems you can identify with. They are uplifting and inspirational in their content, while not always heavily "spiritual." They will be enjoyable and dramatic stories, books you can be proud to read and give to friends. We at Sunrise Books hope you will enjoy the selections chosen for this series. We are always happy for your comments about any of our books.

CONTENTS

Contents

INTRODUCTION

There is a quote from one of George MacDonald's books which I love. It speaks of old gardens with hidden flowers waiting to bloom, and it always reminds me of old forgotten books and authors waiting to be rediscovered by new generations of readers. It speaks of timeless truths, lost sight of perhaps for a season, but abiding still—waiting...waiting...till the time is again ripe for their notice.

In his book *Paul Faber, Surgeon*, MacDonald wrote:

"It is well-enough known that if you dig deep in any old garden, such as this one, ancient—perhaps forgotten—flowers will appear. The fashion has changed, they have been neglected or uprooted, but all the time their life is hid below."

As much as I love old things, and as much as I delight in snooping around musty used bookstores and flipping through dilapidated hundred year old volumes, searching out the book-gardens I encounter in hopes of unearthing a promising tale, Ralph Connor yet escaped my notice for years. Thanks, however, to two good friends who kept pressing him on me, eventually I realized Connor was a literary force to be reckoned with. The sheer sales volume of his original works

7

was impossible to ignore from the historical standpoint alone. As someone interested in publishing, I could not help but be intrigued by Connor.

But as I discovered, there was something far deeper than mere "sales" to give weight to Connor's work. It was my pastor friend who helped drive this home, with his subtle comments about Connor's impact on his own life.

But he didn't stop there. Pretty soon he began giving me some of Connor's titles. "I found this in a used bookstore," he would say. "I already had a copy, so I picked it up and thought you'd like to have it."

What the impact of that gift will be, only time will tell. But I have a feeling it will be something significant. For as I'm sure you know by now, eventually I got hooked. I soon realized myself what my friends had long been telling me: "This guy Ralph Connor wrote some powerful books. We've got to see what can be done to get them back in print and available again to people!" In Connor I found a new literary friend. And my first thought was quite naturally, "How can *I* now share Connor with a wider cross section of people?"

When I find a book or an author whom I think deserves a renewed audience in our generation, at that point begins a long process of thought and prayer and experimentation to discover how best to present such a man's work. In the cases of MacDonald and Connor and Harold Bell Wright, the works of whom I have studied and edited, the original texts are so old that the fashions and writing styles have indeed changed. What I do, therefore, is to "edit" the books for today's reading public, making every attempt before I even begin to get to know the man himself well enough—his thoughts, his attitudes, his feelings, his priorities, his motives for writing, his spiritual bent, his family values, his perspective on salvation and sharing the gospel, etc. Thus, when I sit down at my typewriter, my whole focus is not to intrude *myself* into the text, but rather to present *his* story in a way I think *he* would be proud of today. Of course I play an active not a passive role as an editor; I get in and go over every line, every word. But though I bring my writing and editorial instincts to bear upon it, and use everything I have learned as a writer to make it the best book I can, I still try above all to faithfully represent the original writer, hoping it is *he* that emerges as you read.

It is this process I have gone through in rewriting and editing this series of Ralph Connor novels, tightening up some of Connor's stylistic problems, making the French Canadian and Scottish dialects more readable, updating archaic terminology, occasionally reorganizing a section so that the story flows more smoothly. It is this fine line between "what to alter and what to leave" which presents an editor his essential challenge. Because to be honest, we must admit that times have changed since the 1890's. Many terms Connor would have taken for granted that his early 20th century, largely Canadian, often Scottish audience would have been familiar with as common knowledge are completely outdated today. In certain respects you almost have to be a student of history to really understand the subtleties of these old books. Therefore, there is need for certain changes and explanations if the full impact of the author's original intent is to come through.

How many Americans today, for instance, would appreciate the significance of the song, "Will Ye No Come Back Again" as used so poignantly by Connor in *Black Rock?* Yet that single haunting melody captures the essential mood of Scotland's melancholy history better than any words could, is a tune *every* Scotsman knows by heart, and certainly much of Connor's original Canadian audience would have been familiar with it.

Similarly, without some background, how many of

us would grasp the historical significance to Canada's westward expansion, as well as the spiritual significance in the spread of the gospel throughout the new continent, involved in the work of the young missionaries about which Connor writes in such titles as *Black Rock*, *The Sky Pilot*, *The Prospector*, and others? And how could we possibly know the personal role of the real-life Ralph Connor (a pen name for Winnipeg Presbyterian minister Charles William Gordon) played in his own books, another fact which would have been "common knowledge" to the reader of 1900, but which is lost entirely to us today?

The very title *Sky Pilot* is one whose deeper meaning would entirely elude the contemporary reader at first glance. What was the first thing which came into your mind when you heard the words "Sky Pilot?" If you're like me, the answer is an airplane pilot. That's exactly what I thought.

But *The Sky Pilot* was written four years *before* Kitty Hawk. Connor had no more thought of an airplane pilot when he titled his second book than he did a space ship. The term "pilot" in the nineteenth century meant a "guide," a "director of a course." It was used primarily as the title for the person who steered a ship in dangerous navigation, particularly along coasts, rocky shoals, in and out of harbors, along rivers where hidden rocks had to be avoided. The "pilot" was the most important man aboard a large ship, and had to be well-experienced and knowledgeable about every detail of the course, seen and unseen.

Therefore, when out of the mouth of one of his characters come the words, "...he's just a blanked sky pilot," Ralph Connor was, in a sense, coining an altogether new use of the term to indicate a director, a pilot, through the unknown regions of heavenly waters—a spiritual guide. Such a meaning would have been instantly understood by his readers of 1900 who had never heard of an airplane, but is lost on us today.

For all these reasons, an updated approach is called for. I make what efforts I can—both in the text and by giving backgrounds and explanations of certain things in the Introductions—to assist modern readers to grasp the subtleties intended by the original author. At the same time I try to preserve, in this case, Connor's essential tone, retaining his slightly old-fashioned flavor which has an appeal all its own. I try to update while keeping the fundamental germ of the author's style so that the end result "sounds" like him. These are not modern books, after all, and should not sound like them.

One thing I always look for in an old book is its reality, the sense of history it conveys. That is one of the ingredients I so appreciate in Connor's works—in them one tastes the flavor of Canada's history and the reality of the land. The author was actually there, and through his eyes we can be there too. We feel the pioneering times, we smell the forests, we grow chilly in the snow, the lofty mountain peaks rise before us, and we come to know and love the rugged men who tamed the American West. We feel what it is like to walk the streets of the early settlements and towns, where the cattle roundup, the open prairie, and the law of the gun were the constants of life for many men.

At the same time we are part of the expansion westward of civilization and the penetration of the gospel into these regions by brave young men and women who left all to spread the word of God.

Perhaps more than anything, however, the reality of Connor's writing comes through to me because I know these are real people about whom he is writing. Connor is no mere fictional bystander in his stories. He is telling us, through fictional means, things that many times really occurred. We are thus getting a "first hand account" of life in the Canadian foothills by one who was there.

The words written by Charles Gordon himself about the impact of his "Ralph Connor" pseudonym illuminate the mind of the author concerning his books. In the one publication upon which he used his own name, his own story entitled: *Postscript to Adventure: The Autobiography of Ralph Connor* by Charles William Gordon, the author reflects on the sudden rise in popularity of his books following *Black Rock,* a rise which left him more breathless than anyone, and offers some thoughts of why he thinks it occurred. Read, as Gordon talks about his books, his characters, and about Ralph Connor, now a third person character in Gordon's *own* story:

"I have often tried to analyze the reaction upon my mind of this unique experience. But I have always failed. The comments and criticisms in the magazines and newspapers in both Britain and America were amazingly enthusiastic. I have attempted to explain this reception by a variety of reasons: *Black Rock* and *Sky Pilot* gave an authentic picture of life in the great and wonderful new country in Western Canada, rich in color and alive with movement, the stamping ground of the buffalo and his hunters, the land of the trapper, the Mounted Police and that virile race of men and women, the first pioneers who turned the wild wilderness into civilization. Then, the pictures were from personal experience. I knew the country. I had ridden the ranges. I had pushed through the mountain passes. I had swum my bronco across its rivers. I had met the men—Hi Kendal and Bronco Bill and the rest were friends of mine.

"Another cause of the phenomenal editions of these Ralph Connor books, and a very influential cause, was the fact that though in fiction form they possess a definitely religious motif. Religion is here set forth in its true light as a synonym of all that is virile, straight, honorable and withal tender and gentle in true men and women. And it was this religious motif that startled the vast host of religious folk who up to this time had regarded novel-reading as a doubtful indulgence for Christian people. I have received hundreds of letters expressing gratitude for a novel that presented a quality of religious life that 'red-blooded' men could read and enjoy.

"Of all men, the most surprised at this reception of his books was Ralph Connor himself. He had not the slightest ambition to be a writer. He made little effort after polished literary style. Things just came to him and he put them down. Let me give a quite remarkable instance of that fact. While I was writing *Sky Pilot* it happened that one Sunday morning I was addressing a congregation of children and young people on the general topic, 'The good that pain can do for us,' a difficult enough problem to deal with. As I was standing before that gathering of youngsters there flashed upon my mind a picture of a canyon I knew well in the foothill country and then and there without preparation I told them the story of 'how the canyon got its flowers':

"At first there were no canyons, but only the broad, open prairie. One day the Master of the Prairie...' [and so began, quite spontaneously, the story which the Pilot told to Gwen.]

"I am not ashamed of that canyon picture. One Sunday night after I had preached to a great congregation in Pittsburgh on the theme, 'The Problem of Pain' the minister of the church, after the genial American custom, invited any who desired to come forward and shake hands with the preacher. A thousand people and more passed before me shaking my hand. I remember only one, a girl, pitifully deformed, who paused before me and holding my hand in both of hers lifted a face pale, and bearing the marks of pain, but radiant and said in a low voice, 'Oh, thank you for Gwen!' Then with a quick rush of tears in her eyes, 'the flowers are

13

beginning to grow in my canyon too.' Of the many hundreds I have received I cherish the canyon letters most. They bring me the love and gratitude of those whose canyons of pain have been brightened with the flowers that bloom only in the canyon."[1]

This new edition of Ralph Connor's *The Sky Pilot* has been retitled *Thomas Skyler: Foothills Preacher* as Volume 2 in the Sunrise "Stories of Yesteryear" series. I sincerely hope that you discover a friend in Ralph Connor as I have, and I pray the flowers will blossom in *your* canyon.

I would be happy to hear from any of you. God bless you as you continue to enjoy good books.

Michael Phillips

[1]Charles William Gordon, *Postscript to Adventure: The Autobiography of Ralph Connor*, Canadian Bookman, 1930, pp. 150-52.

PREFACE

The measure of a man's power to help his brother is the measure of the love in his heart and of the faith he has that in the end the good will win. With this love that seeks not its own and this faith that grips the heart of things, he goes out to meet many fortunes, but not that of defeat.

This story is of the people of the Foothill Country; of those men of adventurous spirit, who left homes of comfort, often of luxury, because of the stirring in them to be and to do some worthy thing. It is also the story of those others who, outcast from their kind, sought to find in these valleys, remote and lonely, a spot where they could forget and be forgotten.

The waving skyline of the Foothills was the boundary of their lookout upon life. Here they dwelt safe from the scanning of the world, freed from all restraints of social law, denied the gentler influences of home and the sweet look of a good woman's face. What wonder if, with the new freedom beating in their hearts and ears, some rode fierce and hard the wild trail to the bank of destruction!

The story is, too, of how a man with vision beyond the waving skyline came to them with firm purpose to play the brother's part, and by sheer love of them and by faith in them, win them to believe that life is priceless, and that it is good to be a man.

Ralph Connor
Winnipeg, Canada, 1899

1.
THE COUNTRY OF THE FOOTHILLS

Beyond the great prairies, in the shadow of the Canadian Rockies, lie the Foothills.

For nine-hundred miles the prairie spreads itself out in vast level reaches, and then begins to climb over softly rounded mounds that grow higher and sharper, until at last they break into the jagged points of the mighty mountains. These rounded hills that join the prairies to the mountains form the Foothill Country.

The Foothills extend for only about a hundred miles. But no other hundred miles of the great West are so full of interest and romance. The natural features of that part of the country combine the beauties of both prairie and mountain scenery. There are valleys so wide that the farther side melts into the horizon, and uplands so vast as to suggest the unbroken plains.

Nearer the mountains the valleys dip deep and ever deeper till they narrow into canyons, through which mountain torrents pour their blue-gray waters from glaciers that lie glistening between the white peaks far away. It is here, in these Alberta foothills, where herds of cattle and horses feed on the great ranges. Here are the homes of the ranchmen, in whose wild, free, lonely existence there mingles much of the humor and pathos that combine to make up the romance of life. It is a country whose sunlit hills and shaded valleys reflect themselves in the lives of its people. For nowhere are the contrasts of light and shade more vividly seen than among the ranchmen of the Albertas.

The experiences of my life have confirmed to me the conviction that God sends His rain upon the evil as well as upon the good. Otherwise, I should never have set my eyes upon the Foothill country, nor touched its strangely fascinating life, nor come to know and love one of the most striking men this life has sent my way—the dear old Pilot, as we came to call him long afterward.

I had just finished my first year of college, a year which closed in gloom and left me in much confusion over my future. An invitation from a distant cousin to spend the summer working on a ranch in South Alberta came just at the right moment. For I needed a fresh view of life.

I was wild to go!

Hence it was that I found myself, in the early summer of 1884, attached to a freight train of the Hudson Bay Company, making my way from a little railway town in Montana toward the Canadian border. Our train consisted of six wagons and fourteen yoke of oxen, with three cayuse ponies in the care of a Frenchman and his son of about sixteen.

We made slow enough progress. But every hour of the long day, from the dim gray misty light of dawn to the soft glow of shadowy evening, was full of new delights to me. On the evening of the third day we reached a stopping place at the border, where my cousin Jack Dale met us. I remember well how my heart beat with admiration when I saw the easy grace with which he sailed down off his horse in loose-jointed cowboy style, swinging his own bronco and the little cayuse he was leading for me into the circle of the wagons, seemingly paying no heed to the ropes and freight and other impediments.

He flung himself off before his horse had even come to a stop and gave my hand a grip that made me sure of my welcome. It was years since he had seen a man from home, and the eager joy in his eyes told of long days and nights of lonely yearning for the old days and the old faces. I came to understand this better after my two years' stay among these hills—hills that possess a strange power on some days to waken in a man longings that make his heart grow sick.

Supper that evening consisted of trout cooked over vibrant flame, after which we gathered about the little fire. Jack and the Frenchman smoked and talked, while I lay on my back looking up at the pale steady stars in the deep blue of the cloudless sky, and listened contentedly to the chat between Jack and the other driver. Now and then I asked something but it is a listening silence that draws tales from a Western man, not a barrage of questions. I had already learned this much from my three days of travel. So I lay and listened, and the tales of that night are mingled in my memory with the warm evening lights and the pale stars and the thoughts of home that Jack's coming seemed to bring.

We broke camp the next morning before sun-up and readied ourselves for our fifty mile ride. There was a slight drizzle of rain, though rain and shine were alike to Jack. As I moved toward my ugly-looking little cayuse, I did not altogether like the look of the animal. The feeling was apparently mutual, for as I took him by the bridle, he snorted and twisted about swiftly and stood facing me with his feet planted firmly in front of him as if prepared to reject anything I might be about to do. I tried to approach him with soothing words, but he persistently backed away until we stood looking at each other at the distance of his outstretched neck and my outstretched arm.

Jack had a smile on his face reserved for greenhorns in such predicaments. But he came to my assistance, got the pony by the other side of the bridle, and held him tight while I took a firm grip of the saddlehorn and threw my leg over his back.

The next instant I was flying over his head. My only feeling was one of surprise. The thing was so unexpected, and had happened so quickly. I thought of myself as a fair rider, having had experience with farmer's colts of many different kinds. But this was something quite new. The Frenchman stood looking on with mild interest. Jack was smiling. The boy was grinning with delight.

"I'll ride him," Jack offered, "you take mine. He's quite tame."

But as I saw the laughter rising in the boy, I said, my voice shaking, "No, I'll manage."

I then remounted. But no sooner had I got into the saddle than the pony sprang straight up into the air and landed with his back curved into a bow, his four legs gathered together so rigid that the shock made my teeth rattle.

"Stick to him!" yelled Jack through his shouts of laughter, "You'll make him sick before long. You just have to outlast him."

I remember thinking that unless his insides were somewhat more delicately organized than his external appearance would lead one to suppose, the chances were that the little brute would be the last to succumb to sickness, nor would he tire before me. He kicked and plunged and reared and bucked, now on his front legs, now on his hind legs, while I could only cling to the horn of the saddle for dear life, and it was not many seconds before I was again on my back. Even then the wild little thing continued to buck and plunge about even after I was off his back, as if he were some piece of mechanism that had to run down before it could stop.

By this time I was badly enough shaken to give in entirely, but the laughter of the boy and Jack with his wry grin and the complacent look of the Frenchman stirred my resolve even deeper. I jumped up, seized Jack's riding whip, and, disregarding his remonstrations to try some other horse, sprang again on my steed. And before he could make up his mind as to his line of action, I plied him so vigorously with the rawhide that he set off over the prairie at a full gallop. It did not take long to begin to tire him, and in a few minutes he came round to the camp considerably subdued, somewhat I must admit to my surprise. Jack was highly pleased, and even the stolid face of the Frenchman showed satisfaction.

"Well done!" shouted Jack. "A circus act worth five dollars any day!"

"You bet!" added the Frenchman. "Dat's make pretty beeg fun, eh?"

His comment, it seemed to me, depended upon the point of view, but I agreed, only too glad to have survived the scrap with my honor intact.

When Jack and I were packed and mounted, we bade goodbye to the Frenchman and his son, as they were traveling several miles east to an outpost, while we were to head west. As we rode off I looked back over my shoulder at the pair and waved a final time, wondering if they had been my final link with civilization for some time to come.

All day we followed the trail that wound along the shoulders of the round-topped hills or down their long slopes into the wide, grassy lowlands. Here and there the valleys were cut through by swift, blue-gray rivers, clear and icy cold, while from the hilltops we caught glimpses of little lakes covered with wildfowl. Now and then we saw in the distance what made a small black spot against the green of the prairie, and Jack told me it was some rancher's shack. How remote from the great world and how lonely it seemed!

I shall never forget the summer evening when Jack and I rode into Swan Creek.

I say *into*—but the village was almost entirely one of imagination, in that it consisted only of the Stopping Place, a long log building a story-and-a-half high with stables behind it, and the Store in which the post office was kept and over which the owner lived. These two buildings alone comprised the village. But it was a place of great beauty. On one side the prairie rambled down from the hills and then stretched away in great level reaches into the misty purple of the horizon. On the other it clambered over the round, sunny tops of the hills to the dim blue of the mountains beyond. A more fitting "foothill" location it would be difficult to find than Swan Creek, nestled as it was exactly at the point where the endless prairie and great mountains joined.

In this world where it is often impossible to reach absolute values, and where we are forced to hold things relative to one another, in contrast with the long lonely miles of our ride, the Store and the Stopping Place, with their outbuildings, seemed a very center of life and activity. Some horses were tied to the rail that ran in front of the Stopping Place.

"I guess the Noble Seven are in town!" Jack said, turning to me.

"And who are they?" I asked.

"They are the *life* of Swan Creek," he replied, "and by Jove, this must be a Permit Night."

"What does that mean?" I asked, as we rode up towards the tie rail.

"Well," said Jack in a low tone, for some men were standing about the door, "you see, this is a prohibition country where no alcohol is allowed. But when one of the boys feels as if he were going to have a spell of sickness he gets a permit to bring in a few gallons for medicinal purposes. And of course, the other boys being similarly exposed, he invites them to assist him in taking preventive measures. And," added Jack with a solemn wink, "it is remarkable, in a healthy country like this, how many epidemics come near catching us."

And with this mystifying explanation we dismounted, tied our horses to the rail, and joined the mysterious company of the Noble Seven.

2.

THE COMPANY OF THE NOBLE SEVEN

As we were dismounting, the cries, "Hello, Jack!... Hey, Dale!...What do you say, old Smoke!" in the heartiest of tones, made me see that my cousin was a favorite with the men grouped about the door. Jack simply nodded in reply and then presented me in due form. "My tenderfoot cousin, Ralph Connor, from the big city," he said, with a flourish. Each man in turn gave me a broad welcoming smile and firm shake of the hand. I was surprised at the grace of the bows made me by such rough-dressed, wild-looking fellows; I might have been in a London drawing-room. I was put at ease at once by the kindness of their greetings, on Jack's behalf, and felt at once admitted to their circle, which, to one like me, was usually closed.

What a hardy-looking lot they were!

Brown, spare, sinewy and hard as nails, they appeared like soldiers back from a rigorous campaign. They moved and spoke with an easy, careless air of indifference, but their eyes looked straight out at you, cool and fearless, and you knew they were fit and ready.

That night I was initiated into the Company of the Noble Seven—but I can hardly remember the ceremony, for they drank as they rode, hard and long, and it was only Jack's care that got me safely home that night.

The Company of the Noble Seven was the dominant social force in the Swan Creek country. Indeed, it was the *only* social force Swan Creek knew. Originally consisting of seven young men of the best blood of Britain, "banded together for purposes of mutual improvement and social enjoyment," it had changed its character during the years, but not its name. First, its membership was extended to include "approved colonials," such as Jack Dale and "others of kindred spirit," such as the two cowhands from the Ashley Ranch, Hiram Kendall and "Bronco" Bill Whitely. Then its purposes gradually limited themselves to those of a social nature, chiefly poker-playing and whiskey-drinking. Well born and delicately bred in that atmosphere of culture mingled with a sturdy common sense and a certain high chivalry which surrounds the stately homes of Britain, these young lads, freed from the restraints of custom and surrounding, soon shed all that was superficial in their make-up and stood forth in the naked simplicity of their native manhood. The raw West discovered and revealed the man in them, sometimes to their honor, but often to their shame.

The Chief of the Company was the Honorable Fred Ashley, of the Ashley Ranch, formerly of Ashley Court, England—a big, good-natured man with magnificent physique, a good income from an inheritance at home, and a beautiful wife, daughter of a noble English family—a woman of high prestige who refused the West its claim to alter her tastes. She was, and always vowed to remain, a lady. The couple's childlessness, along with the rigors of life in this untamed wilderness, had taxed Lady Charlotte's noble bearing to its limits.

At the Ashley Ranch the traditions of Ashley Court were preserved as far as possible. The Honorable Fred appeared at the wolf-hunts in riding-breeches and top boots, with hunting crop and English saddle, while in all the appointments of the house the customs of the English home were observed. It was characteristic of western life however, that his two cowboys, Hi Kendall and Bronco Bill, felt themselves quite his social equals, though in the presence of his stately wife they felt rather intimidated. Ashley was a thoroughly good fellow, well up to his work as a cattleman, and too much of a gentleman to feel, much less assert, any superiority of station. He had the largest ranch in the country and was one of the few men making money.

Ashley's most frequent companion was a man they called "The Duke." No one knew his name but every one said he was the son of a lord. And certainly from his style and bearing he might be the son of almost anything high in rank. No one knew anything of his past. He drew "a remittance," but as it was paid through Ashley, no one knew whence it came nor how much it was. He was a perfect picture of a western man. He could rope a steer, bunch cattle, play poker, or drink whiskey to the admiration of his friends and the confusion of his foes, of whom he had a few. As to bronco busting, the virtue *par excellance* of western cattlemen, even Bronco Bill was heard to acknowledge that "he wasn't in it with the Dook," for it was his opinion that he could ride anything that had legs under it, "even if it was a derned centipede."

The Duke lived alone and made a friend of no one, though some men could tell of times when he stood between them and their last dollar, exacting only the promise that no mention should be made of his deed. He had an easy, lazy manner and a slow cynical smile that rarely left his face. Old Latour, who ran the Stopping Place, told me of the one time he had seen the

Duke break into a gentle laugh. A Frenchman on his way north had entered into a game of poker with The Duke, with the result that his six months pay stood in a little heap at his enemy's left hand. The enraged man accused Duke of cheating, and was about to attempt to demolish him with one mighty blow. But Duke, still smiling, and without moving from his chair, caught the descending fist, slowly crushed the fingers open, and steadily drew the Frenchman to his knees, forcing him to cry aloud for mercy. Then it was that The Duke broke into a light laugh and, touching the kneeling Frenchman on his cheek with his fingertips, said, "Look here, my friend, don't play poker till you know how to play the game and know with whom you play." Handing him back the money, he added, "I'll win money at poker, but not your's."

The Duke was by all odds the most striking figure in the Company of the Noble Seven, and his word went farther than that of any other. The man who admired him the most was Bruce, an Edinburgh University man, metaphysical, argumentative, persistent, devoted to the Duke. Indeed, his chief ambition was to be like The Duke, but his attempts at imitation were conspic-uously unsuccessful.

Every mail that reached Swan Creek brought Bruce a letter from home. Usually they took the form of pleas from his mother to return home to Scotland. At first, after I got to know him, he would now and then give me a letter to read, but as the tone became more and more anxious and persuasive he ceased to let me read them, and I was glad enough of this. How he could read those letters and go the pace of the Noble Seven I could not see.

Poor Bruce! He had good impulses, a generous heart. But Permit nights and the hunts and the roundups and the poker and all the wild excesses of the Company were more than he could stand. The singular most remarkable aspects of Bruce's demeanor were his deep contemplations and his tendency toward philosophizing—a characteristic notably out of place in Swan Creek!

Then there were the two Hill brothers, the younger, Bertie, a fair-haired, bright-faced youngster, none too able to look after himself and much inclined to foolishness of all sorts. But he was warmhearted and devoted to his big brother, Humphrey, called "Hump," who had taken to ranching mainly with the idea of looking after his younger brother. And no easy matter that was.

In addition to these, there were two others of the original seven, but by the circumstances of their lives they were now prevented from any more than a nominal connection with the Company. Blake, a typical wild Irishman, had joined the Mounted Police at the Fort, and Gifford had got married and, as Bill said, "was roped tighter'n a steer."

The Noble Company, with the cowboys that helped on the range, along with seven or eight farmers living near the Fort, composed the settlers of the Swan Creek country. A strange medley of people of all ranks and nations it was! But while there, though there were evil-hearted and perhaps evil-living among them, still, for the Noble Company I will say that never have I fallen in with a group of men braver, truer, or of warmer hearts. Vices they had, all too apparent and deadly, but they were due rather to the circumstances of their lives than to the native tendencies of their hearts.

Throughout that summer and the winter following I lived among them, camping on the range with them and sleeping in their shacks, bunching cattle in summer and hunting wolves in winter. And I did not, for I was no wiser than they, refuse my part on "Permit" nights.

But through it all not a man of them ever failed to be true to his standard of honor in the duties of comradeship and brotherhood.

3.
GWEN

The scarcity of population in Swan Creek country allowed newcomers such as myself either a ready acceptance into the community or a prolonged suspicion until proven worthy. For myself, largely because of Jack's influence, I soon found myself in the thick of brotherhood with the general populace.

Indeed, because of my recent academic pursuits, I was prevailed upon to stay that fall and become the schoolmaster of Swan Creek for as long as I happened to stay. The recent arrival of the Muir and Breman families with their housefulls, plus the children of the other farmers, made a school necessary. Some of the men had erected a little long building, and with a few stray books made available by donors, the pupils were assembled whenever there was someone to teach them.

It was the end of the second day of my class when Jack, who had come by to build a tie rail for the children's few ponies, said, "It's a regular shame Gwen'll be having no learning."

29

I had heard of Gwen soon after my arrival, and one day had asked Bill who she was, trying to pin him down to something like an adequate description. Everyone had stories of her. The details were not many, but the impression was vivid. She lived outside Swan Creek, far up in the hills near Devil's Lake. Though she never ventured from her father's ranch, some of the men had had glimpses of her and had come to definite opinions regarding her.

"She's a terror," he said, with slow emphasis, "a holy terror."

"But what is she like? What does she look like?" I asked impatiently.

"Look like?" He considered a moment, then answered, "I dunno."

"Don't know? What do you mean? Haven't you seen her?"

"Yeh! But she ain't like nothin'."

Bill was quite decided upon this point.

I tried again.

"Well, what sort of hair has she got? She's got hair, I suppose?"

"Hair! Well, a few!" said Bill, "Yards of it! Red!"

"Git out!" contradicted Hi who was standing listening. "Red! Tain't no more red than mine!"

Bill regarded Hi's hair critically.

But Hi, paying no attention to Bill, took up the subject with enthusiasm.

"She kin ride—she's a reg'lar buster to ride, ain't she Bill?"

Bill nodded. "She kin bunch cattle an' cut out an' yank a steer up to any cowboy on the range."

"Why, how big is she?"

"Big? Why, she's just a kid! Tain't the bigness of her, it's the nerve. She's got the coldest kind of nerve you ever seen. Hain't she Bill?"

Again Bill nodded.

"Member the day she shot that steer, Bill?" went on Hi.

"What was that?" I asked, eager for a yarn.

"Oh, nuthin'," said Bill.

"Nuthin'!" retorted Hi. "Pretty big nuthin'!"

"What was it?" I urged.

"Oh, Bill here was doing some work at old Meredith's roundup, but he don't speak of it. He's shy, you see," and Hi grinned. "Meredith—that's Gwen's old man."

"Well, there ain't no occasion for your telling that," said Bill disgustedly, and Hi loyally refrained.

So I have never heard the whole story. But from what I did hear, I gathered that Bill, at the risk of his life, had pulled The Duke from under the hoofs of a mad steer, and that little Gwen had, in that coolest possible manner, "sailed in on her bronco," putting two bullets into the steer's head, saving them both from great danger, perhaps even death. Of course Bill could never be persuaded to speak of the incident. A true western man will never hesitate to tell you what he can do, but of what he *has* done he does not readily speak.

The only other item that Hi contributed to the sketch of Gwen was that her temper could flare if the occasion demanded.

"Member young Hill?" he asked his friend.

Bill remembered.

"Didn't she cut into him sudden? Served him right too."

"What did she do?" I asked.

"Cut him across the face with her whip."

"What for?"

"Knockin' about her Indian Joe."

Joe was, as I came to learn, Ponka's son and Gwen's most devoted servant.

"Yes, her temper's quick, but she's good stock,"

added Bill. "She suits me!"

The Duke told me about another side of her character.

"She is a remarkable child," he said one day. "Wild and shy as a coyote, but fearless; with a heart full of passions. Meredith, the Old Timer, has kept his daughter there among the hills. She sees no one but himself and Ponka's Blackfeet relations, who treat her like a goddess and spoil her. She knows their lingo and their ways—goes off with them for a week at a time."

"What! With the Blackfeet?"

"Ponka and Joe go along; but even without them she is as safe as if surrounded by armed guards. But she has given them up for some time now."

"And at home?" I asked. "Has she any education? Can she read or write?"

"No. She can make her own dresses, moccasins, and leggings. She can cook and wash—that is, when she feels in the mood. And she knows all about the birds and beasts and flowers and that sort of thing, but—education! Why, she is hardly civilized!"

"What a shame!" I said. "How old is she?"

"Oh, a mere child, fourteen or fifteen, I imagine; but a woman in many things."

"And what does her father say to all this? Can he control her?"

"Control!" said The Duke, in utter astonishment. "Why nothing in heaven or earth could control *her*. Wait till you see her stand with her proud little head thrown back, giving orders to Joe, and you will never again connect the idea of control with Gwen."

"And how does her father stand her nonsense?" I asked, for I confess I was not much taken with the picture The Duke had drawn.

"Her father simply follows behind her and adores, as do all things that come near her. Still," he added, after a pause, "it *is* a shame, as you say. She ought to know something of the refinements of civilization."

The Duke was silent for a few moments and then added, with some hesitation, "Then, too, she is quite a pagan; never saw a prayer-book, you know."

I questioned Jack, and he told me more of young Gwen, who in reality was sixteen, living in the hills with her father, called by all simply the Old Timer. No one knew much about him except that he had been here the longest and that his opinion in matters of the community carried much weight. No one ventured to disagree with him, for to disagree with the Old Timer was to assign yourself the sure designation of a Tenderfoot. And that was a misfortune only time could repair. It was every tenderfooted newcomer's aim to assume the style and customs of the aristocratic old timers as speedily as possible and forget the date of his own arrival.

At one time the Company of the Noble Seven had sought to bring the Old Timer into its ranks as an honorary member. But he refused to be drawn from his home far up among the hills. He was content there with his Gwen and her half-Indian nurse, Ponka. It was with resentment that the Old Timer watched newcomers venture to Swan Creek. Even the school seemed a threat to him at first, and he wouldn't hear of allowing Gwen to make the long ride.

The Old Timer had no use for the institutions of civilization since that day many years ago when he laid his wife in the lonely grave that could be seen on the shaded knoll just fronting his cabin door. He shrunk from all that reminded him of the great world beyond the run of the prairie, as one shrinks from a sudden touch on an old wound.

4.

MY FIRST VISIT UP THE MOUNTAIN

From the first mention of Gwen and her father, I could not help being intrigued.

I had to meet them, and possibly have a word with the man regarding the education of his daughter. Thus, two mornings later I set out up the mountain to visit the Old Timer and his Gwen.

Jack took me up about halfway, and then, aided by the careful directions Duke had given me which would lead me up the canyon to the Old Timer's cabin, I set off alone.

Up the Swan went the trail, winding ever downward into deeper and narrower ravines, and up to higher sunlit slopes. Then suddenly it settled into a valley which began with great width and narrowed to a canyon, on whose rocky sides grew shrubs and vines, and which were wet with trickling streams from the numerous springs that oozed and gushed from the black, glistening rocks. This canyon was an eerie place of which ghostly tales were told from the old Blackfeet times. But in the warm light of broad day the canyon was a good enough place, cool and sweet, and I lingered on my way until the shadows began to darken its western black sides, though it was barely past noon.

Out of the mouth of the canyon the trail climbed to a wide stretch of prairie that swept up over soft hills and down to the bright gleaming waters of Devil's Lake. In the sunlight the lake lay like a gem radiant with many colors, the far side black in the shadow of the crowding pines, then the middle, deep blue, and purple, and nearer, many shades of emerald that ran to the white, sandy beach. In front stood the ranch buildings, on a slight rising ground and surrounded by a sturdy fence of upright pointed poles. This was the castle of the princess and the Old Timer's private domain. I rode up to the open gate thinking how best to introduce myself.

Suddenly there was an awful roar. My pony shot round upon his hind legs, deposited me sitting upon the ground, and fled down the trail, pursued by two huge dogs that brushed past me as I fell. My shock was interrupted by a peal of laughter, shrill but full of music. Turning, I saw my pupil, as I guessed, standing at the head of a beautiful pinto pony with a heavy cattle whip in her hand. I scrambled to my feet and said, somewhat angrily, I fear:

"What are you laughing at? Why don't you call back your dogs? They will chase my pony beyond all reach."

She lifted her head, shook back her masses of brown-red hair, looked at me as if I were quite beneath contempt and said, "No, they will kill him."

"Then," I said, for now I was angry, "I will kill *them*," pulling at the gun in my belt.

"Then," *she* said, and for the first time I noticed her blue-black eyes with gray rims, "I will kill you," and she whipped out an ugly-looking revolver.

From her face I had no doubt that she would not hesitate to do as she had said. I changed my tactics, for I was anxious about my pony, and said, with my best smile, "Can't you call them back? Won't they obey you?"

Her face changed in a moment.

"Is it your pony? Do you love him very much?"

"Dearly!" I said, persuading myself of a sudden affection for the cranky little brute.

She sprang on her pinto and set off down the trail. She whistled shrilly, and called to her dogs, "Down, Wolf! Back, Loo!" but, running low, with long, stretched bodies, they did not heed her but sped on, gaining on the pony that now circled toward the pinto. As they drew near in their circling, the girl urged her pinto to meet them, loosening her lariat as she went. As the pony neared the pinto he slowed; immediately the nearer dog gathered herself in two short jumps and sprang, the lariat whirled round the girl's head and fell swift and sure about the dog's neck, and the next moment she lay choking upon the prairie. Her mate paused, looked back, and gave up the chase. But vengeance overtook her, for like one possessed, the girl began beating them with her whip, until, in pity for the brutes, I intervened.

"They shall do as I say or I shall kill them! I shall kill them!" she cried, raging and stamping.

"Better shoot them," I suggested, pulling out my pistol.

Immediately she flung herself upon the one that moaned and whined at her feet, crying:

"If you dare!" Then she burst into passionate sobbing. "You bad Loo! You bad, dear old Loo! But you *were* bad—you *know* you were bad!" and so she went on with her arms about Loo's neck till Loo, whining and quivering with love and delight, threatened to go quite mad, and Wolf, standing majestically near, broke into short howls of impatience for his turn of caressing. They made a strange group, those three wild things, equally fierce and passionate in hate and in love.

Suddenly the girl remembered me, and standing up she said, half ashamed, "They always obey *me*. They are *mine*, but they kill any strange thing that comes in through the gate. They are allowed to."

"It is not a pleasant whim."

"What?"

"I mean, isn't that dangerous to strangers?"

"Oh, no one ever comes alone, except The Duke. And they keep off the wolves."

"The Duke comes, does he?"

"Yes!" and her eyes lit up. "He is my friend. He calls me his 'princess,' and he teaches me to talk and tells me stories—oh, wonderful stories! You must be the new schoolteacher?" She then said suddenly.

"Yes," I answered a bit surprised, "How did you know?"

"Duke told me about you."

"I see."

"Do you know my father?" she asked.

"I've seen him once or twice down at Swan Creek," I said.

"Come," she said rising, "I'll take you to him."

I looked in wonder at her face, so gentle, so girlish, and tried to think back to the picture of the girl who a few moments before had so coolly threatened to shoot me and had so furiously beaten her dogs.

I kept her talking of The Duke as we walked back to the gate, all the time watching her face. It was not beautiful; it was too thin, and the mouth was too large. But the teeth were good, and the eyes looked straight at you; true eyes and brave. Her hair was her glory. Red it was, in spite of Hi's denial, but of such marvelous, indescribable shade that in certain lights, as she rode over the prairie, it streamed behind her like a purple banner. A most confusing and bewildering color, but quite in keeping with the nature of its owner.

37

She gave her pinto to Joe and, standing at the door, welcomed me with a dignity and graciousness which made me think that The Duke was not far wrong when he named her "Princess."

The door opened on the living room. It was a long apartment, with low ceiling and walls of hewn logs chinked and plastered and all beautifully whitewashed and clean. The tables, chairs, and benches were all homemade. On the floor were magnificent skins of wolf, bear, musk ox, and mountain goat. The walls were decorated with heads and horns of deer and mountain sheep, eagles' wings, and a beautiful breast of a loon, which Gwen had shot and of which she was very proud. At one end of the room a huge stone fireplace stood radiant in its summer decorations of ferns and grasses and wild-flowers. At the other end a door opened into another room, smaller and richly furnished.

Everything was clean and well kept. Every nook, shelf, and corner was decked with flowers and ferns from the canyon.

A strange house it was, full of curious contrasts, but it fitted this quaint child that welcomed me with such gracious courtesy.

Before I left late in the afternoon, full of the simple hospitality of this humble cabin and its two occupants, it was agreed that, though she would not set foot in the schoolhouse, I would yet be permitted to teach Gwen here, if I was determined to make the trip.

I said I would come twice a week. Then I left this mountain to make my way back through the canyon now filled with shadows, feeling that I had won a great victory.

5.

THE COMING OF THE PREACHER

Thus it was that, happily settled as schoolmaster and feeling no inclination to cut my stay in the foothills short, I came into contact with the first newcomer to arrive in the area after myself—and that by way of letter. The person I refer to is the man who would come to have such a marked influence, not only on the Swan Creek area, but upon the entire Alberta Foothills region—the foothills preacher.

The letter which preceded his arrival was brought to me by the Hudson Bay freighters early one summer evening and bore the simple inscription:

The Schoolmaster
Public School
Swan Creek,
Alberta

There was altogether a fine air about the letter, which was signed, *Thomas Skyler*. His letter took me into his confidence. He was glad to know that there was a school and a teacher in Swan Creek, for a school meant children, in whom his soul delighted; and in the teacher he would find a friend, and without a friend he could not live. He told me that though he had volunteered for this far-away mission field he was not much of a preacher and he was not at all sure that he would succeed. But he meant to try, and he was thankful at the prospect of having one sympathizer at least, and would I be kind enough to put in some conspicuous place the enclosed notice, filling in the blanks as I thought best?

> *Religious service will be held at Swan Creek*
> *in   at   o'clock.*
> *All are cordially invited.*
> *Thomas Skyler*

My first impression of the man was favorable. I liked the modesty of his letter, and its hopeful assumption of my sympathy and cooperation.

But at the same time, I found myself in a quandary. For Sunday was the day set for the great baseball match, when those from "Home," as they fondly called the land across the sea from which they had come, were to "wipe the face of the earth" with all comers. Besides this conflict, a church service in Swan Creek would be such an innovation that I was sure, like all innovations suggesting the approach of the East not to mention hinting at reform, it would by no means be welcome.

Nevertheless, immediately under the notice of the "Grand Baseball Match" for a week from Sunday at 2:30, *Home vs. the World,* I tacked on the door of the Stopping Place the announcement:

> *Religious Service will be held at Swan Creek,*
> *in the Stopping Place Parlor, a week from*
> *Sunday, immediately upon the conclusion of*
> *the baseball match.*
> *All are cordially invited.*
> *Thomas Skyler*

There was a strange incongruity in the two announcements, and an unconscious challenge as well.

All the next day, which was Saturday, and indeed throughout the following week, I kept a watchful eye on the notice, and was amused by the reactions and comments it produced. It represented the advance wave of the great ocean of civilization which many of the men had been glad to leave behind—some could have wished forever.

For others, however, the coming of a church service was welcome. To Robert and Alda Muir, one of the newly arrived Scottish farm families, the notice was a harbinger of good. It stood for progress, markets, and a higher price for land, though the tight Scotsman wondered "hoo he wad be keepit up." But his hard-working and quick-spoken little wife hooted his scruples, and, thinking of her children, welcomed with unmixed satisfaction the coming of the "meenister." Her satisfaction was shared by all the mothers and most of the fathers in the settlement.

But as was true with a good many issues, the opinion on the side of the farm folks was keenly at variance with that of the more primitive cowhands, most of whom, and especially that rollicking and roistering crew, the Company of the Noble Seven, viewed the missionary's coming with varying degrees of animosity. It would no doubt mean an attempted limitation of freedom in their wild and reckless living. The "Permit" nights would not, to say the least, avoid being subject to criticism. The Sunday wolf hunts and horse races, with their accompanying delights, would now be pursued under the watchful eye of the Church.

Of all the "Company" Bruce seemed most bitter about the advent of the minister. He was himself the son of an Edinburgh minister, and swore that the joy of "letting a fellow do as he dern well pleased" would be gone. He thought it to be an attempt "to reimpose an

antiquated and bigoted traditionalism on their freedom."

And the rest of the Company, while not taking so
decided a stand, were agreed that the establishment of
a church was an objectionable and unnecessary proceeding.

As for Hi Kendall and Bronco Bill, they had no opinion one way or the other. Their dozen years in Montana
had proved to them that a church was a luxury of civilization the West might do well without. Certainly its
effect on them could hardly be less remote.

The Old Timer, whose opinion was highly valued,
thought of the church as he did the school, yet another
encroachment of civilization. I stood by one day when
he was down from the mountain, as he read carefully
the notice. He thought for a second, then turned to me
and said with resignation, "It's getting pretty crowded
'round Swan Creek these days. I guess it's about time
for Gwen and me to move on."

"Why?" I said in surprise. For someone as perma-
nent as the Old Timer to move away was unthinkable.
His grazing range was certainly still more than ample
for his herd.

"Oh, this blamed...what's hizname?"

He turned to look again at the notice. "This Sky fellow. Come here to try and guide us...lead our lives. We
done fine without him. Settled this land just fine. Why
can't such fellows keep their religion outta where it
ain't wanted?"

His eyes squinted as he looked once again at the
notice, reading the name aloud, "Thomas Skyler. Huh!
Skyler, just a blanked Sky Pilot if you ask me. Come to
pilot our lives right out from under us!"

"Well," I said, "I don't suppose you have to listen to
him, but to leave Swan Creek? You can't do that. Think
of Gwen. I'm making progress in her reading. Be a
real shame to stop her studies."

He thought for a minute and said, "Dunno. Ain't yet figgered that out."

Then he caught sight of the hills over my back and said, "Ah, what's the use? She wouldn't leave her foothills. She loves the hills like a man loves a woman."

I waited for a moment, then said, "Well, you don't have to decide now anyway," realizing that the one thing an old timer hates to do is make any change in his mode of life. "Besides, maybe he won't stay."

He caught at this eagerly. "That's so! There ain't much to keep him here. These people got no use for a church. If a man wants God, all he got to do is look up at them hills."

He turned and walked on towards his horse. I thought after him for a moment about the tragedy of his wife's death and I found myself wondering about his future—and Gwen's. And I made up my mind that if the missionary were the right sort, his coming might not be a bad thing even for the Old Timer. Nor for others in this Swan Creek community.

6.
THE PILOT'S MEASURE

The Old Timer's brand "Sky Pilot" caught hold. Before the minister's coming the conversations around Swan Creek took on the air of speculation about what sort this Skyler fellow, this "Sky Pilot" would be.

It was Hi Kendall who first announced the arrival of the Sky Pilot. I was standing at the door of my school, watching the children ride off home on their ponies, when he came loping along on his bronco in the loose-jointed cowboy style.

"Well," he drawled, bringing his bronco to a dead stop in a single bound, "he's lit."

"Lit? Who?" I asked.

"Your blanked Sky Pilot, and he's a beaut! A pretty kid—looks too tender for this climate. Best not let him out on the range," Hi said in disgust.

"What's the matter with him?"

"Why, *he* ain't no parson! I don't go much on parsons, but when I calls for one I don't want no bantam chicken. No sireee! When I'm laid out in my coffin fixin' to be planted, I don't want no pink-and-white complected

44

nursery kind sayin' words over me. If you're going to bring along a parson, at least bring him with his eye-teeth cut and his tail feathers on."

The outlook for Skyler wasn't encouraging. With the exception of the Muirs and the Scottish farmers, who really counted for little, nobody wanted him. To most of the reckless young-bloods of the Company of the Noble Seven his presence was an offense; to others simply a nuisance, while the Old Timer regarded his coming with something like dismay. Then to top it all off, Hi's impression of his personal appearance was not favorable.

My first sight of the man did not reassure me. He was slight, very young, very innocent, with a face which seemed strangely out of place among the rough, hard faces that were to be seen in the Swan Creek Country. It was not a weak face, however. The forehead was high and square, the mouth firm, and the eyes luminous, of some dark color—violet, if there is such a color in eyes—dreamy or sparkling, according to his mood; eyes for which a woman might find use, but which, in a missionary's head, appeared to me one of those extraordinary wastes of which Nature seems sometimes guilty.

He was gazing far away into space infinitely beyond the Foothills and the blue line of the mountains behind them. It was clear these surroundings were new to him. He turned to me as he dismounted and tied his horse to the rail.

"It is glorious," he almost panted with eyes alight and face glowing. "You see this every day?"

Then, coming to himself, he walked eagerly toward me, stretching out his hand. "You are the school-master, I know," he said without waiting for an answer, then went on, "You know teaching is a wonderful thing. I wanted to be a teacher, but I never could lead the boys on in their studies. They always got me telling them tales. I was awfully disappointed. I am trying the next best thing. I fancy preaching is not so much different from teaching. But I don't think I can preach very well. Ah, but I think teaching is splendid. You must be very happy in your endeavor here?"

I had thought to be somewhat aloof with him, but his open admiration of me softened this intention, and as he talked on, his enthusiasm and charm of manner and luminous eyes made him perfectly irresistible. Before I was aware of it I was listening to his plans for working his mission with eager interest. So eager in fact, that I found myself asking him to tea in my shack. But he declined, saying:

"I'd like to, but I think Latour expects me at the Stopping Place. But why don't you ride on in with me."

So we rode into town rather slowly as Skyler quietly watched the landscape around us. A landscape, I reckoned, I was all too quickly getting used to.

Latour welcomed us with his grim old face wreathed in unusual smiles. It was clear he had already talked to Skyler.

"I've got it, Latour!" he cried as he entered, "I've remembered," and he broke into the beautiful French-Canadian song *A la Claire Fontaine*, to old Latour's nearly tearful delight.

As he finished the verse he said, "Do you know I first heard that down the Mattawa?" And away he went into a story of an experience with French-Canadian raftsmen, mixing up his French and English in so charming a manner that Latour, who in his younger days long ago had been a shantyman himself, hardly knew what to think.

After tea I proposed a ride out to see the sunset from the small hills just to the north of town. Latour, with unexampled generosity, offered his own cayuse, "Louis."

"I can't ride well," protested The Pilot.

"Ah! dat's good ponee, Louis," urged Latour. "He's quiet lak wan leetle mouse; he's ride lak—what you call?—wan horse-on-de-rock."

Under this persuasion the pony was accepted.

That evening I saw the Swan Creek country with new eyes—through the luminous vision of this new Sky Pilot. We rode up the trail by the side of the Swan till we came to the ravine, dark and full of mystery.

He looked lingeringly into the deep shadow and asked, "Anything live down there?"

"Coyotes and wolves, and, to hear the Old Timer tell it, ghosts."

He laughed.

Then, we took the porcupine trail and climbed for about two miles to the top of the rising ground. There we stayed and watched the sun take his nightly plunge into the sea of mountains, now dimly visible.

Behind us stretched the prairie, sweeping out level to the sky and cut by the winding ravine of the Swan. Great long shadows from the hills were lying across its yellow face, and far at the distant edge the gray haze was deepening into purple. Before us lay the hills, softly curving like the shoulders of great sleeping giants, their tops still bright, but the separating valleys full of shadow. And there, far beyond them, up against the sky, was the line of the mountains—blue, purple, and gold, according as the light fell on them. The sun had taken his plunge, but had left behind his robes of saffron and gold.

We stood long without a word of movement, filling our hearts with the silence and beauty, till the gold in the west grew dim. High above us the night was stretching her star-pierced, blue canopy, and drawing slowly up from the east over the prairie and over the sleeping hills the soft folds of a purple haze. The great silence of the dying day had fallen upon the world and held us fast.

"Listen," he said in a low tone, pointing to the hills. "You can almost hear them breathe!" And, looking at the curving shoulders, I fancied I could see them slowly heaving as if in deep sleep, and I was quite sure I could hear them breathe. I was under the spell of his voice and all nature seemed alive.

We rode back to the Stopping Place in silence, except for a word of mine now and then which he heeded not. With hardly a good night, he left me at the door. I turned away feeling as if I had been in a strange country and among strange people.

How would he do as a preacher? How would he do with the Swan Creek folk? Could he make them see the hills breathe? Would he show them unseen realities through the use of mere words? Would they feel as I felt under his voice and eyes? What a curious mixture he was.

The next few days would give some evidence. The service was scheduled; it would not be changed. But I felt it a pity to be in conflict with the baseball match. I determined to speak to some of the men in the morning about changing the game.

Hi might be disappointed in his appearance, but as I turned into my shack and thought over my last two hours, I began to think that Hi might be mistaken in his measure of The Pilot.

7.
SKYLER'S FIRST SUNDAY

I was determined to try to have the baseball match postponed.

To the easy going men of Swan Creek one day was as much of a holiday as another. But when I suggested a change in the day, The Duke simply raised his eyebrows an eighth of an inch and said, "Can't see why the day should be changed," and all the others followed his lead.

That Sunday was a day of contrasts. The Old and New, the East and West. The baseball match was played with great vigor and profanity. The expression on Skyler's face, as he stood watching was a curious mixture of surprise, interest, and pain. He was a sensitive young man and the utter disregard of all he considered sacred couldn't help but be disconcerting. It was his first close view of practical, skeptical living without the confines of any religion. Skepticism in a book did not disturb him; he could write more words to put down against it. But here it was alive—and even to an extent appealing. I could see the attraction in those

dark eyes, for the colorful garb of the men, the loose-
ness of their lives, and their western swing had captured his imagination. It was clearly causing him a
fierce internal struggle.

The match went on uproariously to a finish with the
champions from the old country going down to defeat,
chiefly due to the work of Hi and Bronco Bill as
pitcher and catcher.

After the game, as was the custom, the men retired
to the Stopping Place where as Hi put it, "the boys
were takin' their whuppin' good and calm."

The celebration was in full swing when Skyler walked in. A silence immediately fell upon the room. His
face still bore the pain of the day as he walked up to
the bar. He stood a moment hesitating and looking
round upon the faces flushed and hot that were now
turned toward him in curious defiance. He noticed the
look and it pulled him together. He walked through the
crowds and up to the bar, behind which old Latour
stood, and asked in a clear voice:

"Is this the room you said we might have for a service?"

Latour shrugged his shoulders and said, "I have no
other."

The lad paused for an instant, then, lifting a pile of
hymn books he had near him on the counter, he said,
"Gentlemen, Mr. Latour has graciously allowed me
this room for a religious service. It will give me great
pleasure if you will all join," and immediately he handed a book to Bronco Bill who, surprised, took it as if he
did not know what to do with it. The others were as
much at a loss and found themselves following Bill's
lead. They each took one, until a book was offered to
Bruce. He refused it, saying roughly, "No—I don't
want that thing. I got no use for it."

Skyler flushed and drew back. But immediately, as
if unconsciously, The Duke, who was standing near,

stretched out his hand and said with a courteous bow, "I thank you, I should be glad of one." Most of the men stood quietly at The Duke's unexpected gesture, not sure what to make of it.

"Thank you," replied Skyler simply as he handed him a book.

The men seated themselves on the bench that ran round the room, or leaned up against the counter. Most of them by now were taking off their hats. Just then in came Muir and behind him his little wife.

In an instant The Duke was on his feet, and the rest of the hats came off.

The missionary stood up at the bar and announced the hymn, "Jesus, Lover of My Soul." The silence that followed was broken by the sound of a horse galloping. A buckskin pony flew past the window and in a moment the Old Timer appeared at the door. He was about to stride in when the unusual sight of a row of men sitting solemnly with hymn books in their hands held him fast at the door.

He gazed in on the men, then at the missionary, then back at the men, and stood speechless.

Suddenly from the bar there was a resonant but high pitched laugh and all turned to see Skyler in a fit of laughter. The shock dealt the final blow to any lingering ideas of religious propriety they might have had about them; the contrast between his honest laughing face and the amazed look of the shaggy old man in the doorway was too much for them, and one by one they gave way to roars of laughter. The Old Timer, however, kept his face unmoved, strode up to the bar and nodded to old Latour, who served him his drink, which he took at a gulp.

"Here old man!" called out Bill, "get into the game; here's your deck," he said, offering him his book. But the missionary was ahead of him, and with a polite grace he handed the Old Timer a book and pointed him to a seat.

I shall never forget that service. As a religious affair it was a dead failure, but somehow I think Skyler made his point, and it was not wholly a defeat. The first hymn was sung chiefly by the preacher and Mrs. Muir, whose voice was very high, with only one or two of the men softly whistling an accompaniment. The second hymn was better, and then came the Lesson, the story of the feeding of the five thousand.

As Skyler finished the story, Bill, who had been listening with great interest, said, "I say, pard, but I think it's time for me to call you."

"I beg your pardon?" said the startled preacher.

"You're givin' us quite a song and dance now, ain't you?"

"I don't understand," was the puzzled reply.

"Now how many men did you say was in the crowd?" asked Bill with a judicial air.

"Five thousand."

"And how much grub?"

"Five loaves and two fishes," answered Bruce in a bored voice before the missionary could speak.

"Well," drawled Bill, with the air of a man who has reached a conclusion, "that's a little too unusual for me. Why, it ain't natural."

Bruce grinned, "Right you are my boy. It's deucedly unnatural."

"Not for Him," said the missionary quietly. "I'm afraid there are a great many things I don't understand, and I'm not good at arguing..."

At this there were shouts of "Yes, go on!...Fire ahead! ...Tell him!" But he said, "I think we will close the service with a hymn now."

His frankness and modesty, and his respectful, courteous manner gained the sympathy of the men, so that all joined heartily in singing, "Sun of My Soul."

In the prayer that followed his voice grew stronger. The words were very simple, and the petitions were mostly for light and strength. With a few words of remembrance of "those in our homes far away who think of us and pray for us and never forget," this strange service was brought to a close.

After the missionary had left, the whole affair was discussed with great warmth. Hi Kendall thought, "that there Sky Pilot didn't have no fair chance," maintaining that when he was "ropin' a steer he didn't want no fool tenderfoot to be shovin' in his rope like Bill done." But Bill steadily maintained his position that "the story of that there picnic was a little too far-fetched" for him. Bruce had taken The Duke aside and was trying to beguile him into a discussion of the physics and metaphysics of the case. But The Duke refused to be drawn into it, saying he preferred poker himself, if Bruce cared to take a hand. And so the evening went, with the theological discussion by Hi and Bill in a friendly spirit in one corner, while the others for the most part played poker.

When the missionary returned late there were only a few left in the room, among them The Duke and Bruce, who was drinking steadily and losing money. The missionary's presence seemed to irritate Bruce considerably and he played even more recklessly than usual, swearing deeply at every loss. At the door Skyler stood looking up into the night sky and humming softly "Sun of My Soul," and after a few minutes The Duke joined in humming a bass to the tune till Bruce could contain himself no longer.

"I say," he called out, "this isn't any blanked prayer-meeting, is it?"

The Duke ceased humming. He looked at Bruce, and said quietly, "Well, what's got into you? What's the trouble?"

"Trouble?" shouted Bruce. "I don't see what hymn singing has to do with a poker game. That's the trouble."

The Duke looked at him with affectionate concern. "Oh, I see. I beg your pardon. Was I singing? I didn't even realize it." Then after a pause he added, "You're quite right. I say, Bruce, let's quit. Something has got on your nerves." He coolly swept his pile of winnings into his pocket and rose to leave.

Bruce left the table cursing, took another drink, and went unsteadily out to his horse, and soon we heard him ride away into the darkness, singing snatches of the hymn and swearing the most awful oaths.

The missionary's face was white. The atmosphere of drink and cursing and gambling and sacrilege was all new and horrible to him.

"Will he get safely home?" he asked The Duke.

"Don't you worry, youngster, he'll get along fine."

The luminous eyes grew hard and bright as he looked The Duke in the face.

"But, I *shall* worry. You ought to worry more."

"Ah," said The Duke, raising his brows and smiling gently on the bright young face lifted up to his. "I didn't notice that I had asked your opinion."

"If anything should happen to him," replied the missionary, "I should consider you largely responsible."

"That would be kind," said The Duke, still smiling. But after a moment's steady gaze into the missionary's eyes he nodded his head quietly and turned away.

The missionary turned to me as I stood next to the bar observing. "They may have made me look foolish this afternoon," he said, "but thank God I know now they are wrong. I don't understand everything, but I know it's true! Men can't live without Him and be men!"

And long after I went to my shack that night I saw before me the eager face and those piercing eyes and heard again that triumphant cry, "I know it's true! Men can't live without Him and be men!" And I knew that though his first Sunday ended somewhat in defeat there must be victory yet awaiting him.

8.
HIS SECOND WIND

The first weeks were not pleasant for Skyler. His initial sense of failure dampened his fine enthusiasm, one of his chief charms. The Noble Seven ignored or laughed at him, according to their mood. Bruce often patronized him. And, worst of all, the Muirs pitied him. It was this last that brought him low, and I was glad to see his reaction. I find it hard to put up with a man who enjoys pity.

It was Hi Kendall who restored him, though Hi had no thought of doing so good a deed. Another baseball match was on with The Porcupines from near the Fort. To Hi's disgust and team's dismay, Bill, who always pitched, was laid up with a virus.

"Try The Pilot, Hi," said someone teasing him as the teams assembled on the coarse field.

Hi looked glumly across at Skyler standing some distance away, then called out, holding up the ball:

"Can you play?"

As his answer Skyler merely held up his hands for a catch. Hi tossed him the ball easily. The ball came back so quickly that Hi was hardly ready, and the jar amazed him.

"I'll take him," he said doubtfully, and the game began. Hi fitted on his catcher's mask and waited.

"How do you like them?" asked Skyler.

"Hot!" said Hi. "I hain't got no gloves to burn."

The Preacher turned his back, swung off one foot on to the other and released his ball.

"Strike!" called the umpire.

"You bet!" said Hi, with emphasis, but his face was a picture of dawning delight.

Again Skyler went through his motions on the mound, sent in a fast one, and again the umpire called:

"Strike!"

He returned the ball without holding it and set himself for the third pitch. Once more that disconcerting swing and the whip-like action of the arm, and for the third time the umpire called:

"Strike! Batter out!"

"That's the way," yelled Hi.

The Porcupines couldn't believe what had happened. Hi looked at the ball in his hand, then at the slight figure of the minister.

"I say! Where do you get it?"

"What?" asked Skyler innocently.

"That gait!"

"The what?"

"The gait! The speed, you know!"

"Oh! I used to play a bit at Princeton."

"Did, eh? What the tarnation did you quit for?"

He evidently regarded the exchange of proficiency at baseball for the study of religion as a serious error in judgment, and every inning of the game confirmed this opinion in him. At bat Skyler did not particularly shine, but he made up for his light hitting by his base-running. He was fast and knew the game thoroughly.

He was keen, eager, and intense in play, and before the innings were half over he was recognized as the best all-round man on the field. On the pitcher's mound he puzzled the Porcupines till they grew desperate and hit wildly and blindly, amid the jeers of the spectators. Their bewilderment was equaled only by the enthusiasm of Hi and his nine, and when the game was over the score stood 18 to 7 in favor of the Home team. They carried The Pilot off the field.

From that day Skyler was a new man. He had won the unqualified respect of Hi Kendall and most of the others, for he could beat them at their own game and still be modest about it. Once more his enthusiasm came back. The Duke rather disliked baseball and was not present to witness his triumph. Bruce was there, however, but took no part in the general acclaim. Indeed, he seemed rather annoyed with Skyler's sudden leap into favor. Certainly his hostility to the preacher and all that he stood for was none the less open and bitter.

Bruce's rancor was more than usually marked at the service held on the following Sunday. It was, perhaps, worsened by the open and delighted approval of Hi, who was prepared to back up anything Skyler would venture to say. Bill, who had not witnessed Skyler's performance in the game but had only Hi's enthusiastic report to go on, still preserved his judicial air. Bill had great confidence in Hi's opinion of baseball, but was not prepared to surrender his right of private judgment in matters theological, so he waited for the sermon before committing himself to any more general approval.

This service was an undoubted success. The singing was hearty, and the men fell into a more reverent attitude during prayer. The theme, too, was one that gave little room for skepticism. It was the story of Zaccheus, and storytelling was Skyler's strong point. Vivid portraitures of the outcast, the shrewd converted publican, and the supercilious, self-complacent Pharisee were drawn with a few deft touches. A single sentence transferred them to the Foothills and arrayed them in cowboy garb. Bill was none too sure of himself, but Hi, with delightful winks, was indicating Bruce as the Pharisee, to the latter's scornful disgust. The preacher must have noticed, for with a very clever turn the Pharisee was shown to be the kind of man who likes to fit faults upon others. Then Bill, digging his elbows into Hi's ribs, said in an audible whisper:

"Say, pardner, how does it fit now?"

"You git out!" answered Hi, indignantly, but his confidence in his interpretation of the application was shaken. When Skyler came to describe the Master and His place in that ancient group, we in the Stopping Place parlor fell under the spell of his eyes and voice, and our hearts were moved within us. That great personality was made very real. Hi was quite subdued by the story and the picture. Bill was perplexed; it was all new to him; but Bruce was mainly irritated. To him it was all old and filled with memories he hated to face. At any rate he was unusually savage that evening, drank heavily and went home late, raging and cursing at things in general and the preacher in particular—for Skyler, in a timid sort of way, had tried to quiet him and help him to his horse.

"Ornery sort o' beast now, ain't he?" said Hi, with the idea of comforting The Pilot, who stood sadly looking after Bruce disappearing in the night.

"No! No!" he answered, quickly, "not a beast, but a brother."

"Brother! Not much, if I know my relations!" answered Hi, disgustedly.

"The Master thinks a good deal of him," was the earnest reply.

"Git out!" said Hi, "You don't mean it! Why," he

added decidedly, "he's more stuck on himself than that mean old cuss you was tellin' about this afternoon, and without half the reason."

But Skyler only said, kindly, "Don't be hard on him, Hi," and turned away, leaving Hi and Bill gravely discussing the question, with the aid of several drinks of whiskey. They were still discussing when, an hour later, they too disappeared into the darkness that swallowed up the trail to Ashley Ranch.

That was the first of many such services which began to be held in the schoolhouse. The preaching was always of the simplest kind. Skyler avoided abstract questions and stuck to the concrete, dressing those wonderful Bible tales in modern western garb. Bill and Hi were more than ever his friends and the latter was heard exultantly to exclaim to Bruce:

"He ain't much to look at as a parson, but he's a-ketchin' his second wind, and 'fore long you won't see him for dust."

9.
THE LAST OF THE PERMIT SUNDAYS

Winter came and went, and spring roundups were now all over and Bruce had nothing to do but to loaf about the Stopping Place, drinking old Latour's bad whiskey and making himself a nuisance. The combination seemed to affect not only Bruce's descending spirits, but his health as well. He did not look good. The Pilot tried to win over his friendship with loans of books and magazines and other courtesies, but to little avail.

The skeptic would be decent for a day and then break forth in violent arguments against religion and all who held to it. He sorely missed The Duke, who was away south on one of his periodic journeys, of which no one knew anything or dared to ask. The Duke's presence always steadied Bruce and took the rasp out of his manners. It was rather a relief to everyone that he was absent from the next fortnightly service.

"I just can't seem to get through to Bruce," Skyler said to me, after the service, "I'd give anything to help him."

"If he doesn't quit his nonsense," I replied, "he'll soon be past helping. He doesn't go out on his range much these days, his few cattle wander everywhere, his shack is in a terrible state, and he is going to pieces, miserable fool that he is."

"You are too hard on him," said Skyler, his eyes upon me.

"Hard? But isn't it true!" I answered.

"Yes, but can he help it." Is it all his fault?" he replied, with his steady eyes still looking into me.

"Whose fault is it, then?"

"What about the Noble Seven? Have they anything to do with this?" His voice was quiet, but there was an intensity in it.

"Well," I said, rather weakly, "a man ought to look after himself."

"Yes!—and his brother when necessary."

Then he went on:

"What have any of you done to help him? The Duke could have pulled him up a year ago if he had been willing to deny himself a little, and so with all of you. You all do just what pleases you regardless of any other, and so you help bring one another down."

I could not find anything to say, for, though his voice was quiet and low, his eyes were glowing and his face was alight with the fire that burned within. I felt like one convicted of a crime. This was certainly a new notion for the West; an uncomfortable doctrine to practice, but in Skyler's way of viewing things difficult to escape. There would be no end to one's responsibility if you took the Pilot's words of helping others completely seriously. I refused to think it out.

Within two weeks we *were* thinking it out, however.

The Noble Seven were to have a great celebration at the Hill brothers' ranch. The Duke had just gotten home from his southern trip a little more weary-looking than when he left, but vowed to be present. The blow-out was to be held on Permit Sunday, the alternate to the Preaching Sunday, which was a concession to Skyler, and had been secured chiefly through the influence of Hi and his baseball nine. Hi put it rather graphically. "The devil takes his innin's one Sunday and The Sky Pilot the next," adding emphatically, "he hain't done much scoring' yit, but my money's on The Pilot!" Bill was more cautious and preferred to await developments.

And developments were rapid.

The Hill brothers' gathering was unusually raucous. Several Permits had been requisitioned, and whiskey and beer abounded. Races all day, poker all night, and drinks of various brews both day and night, with varying impromptu amusements—such as shooting the horns off wandering steers—were the social amenities indulged in by the noble company.

On Monday evening I rode out to the ranch, urged by Skyler, who was anxious that someone should look after Bruce in the midst of the revelry.

"I don't belong to them yet," he said, "but you do. They won't resent your coming."

Nor did they. They were sitting around a poker table, and welcomed me with a shout.

"Hey schoolteacher! Where's your preacher friend?" asked Bruce cynically.

"Where you ought to be, if you could get there—at home," I replied, nettled at his insolent tone.

"Strike one!" called out Hi, enthusiastically, not approving Bruce's attitude toward his friend, The Preacher. The others present chuckled lightly.

"Don't be so serious," said Bruce, after the laugh had passed, "have a drink."

He was flushed, and very noisy. The Duke, at the head of the table, looked a little harder than usual, but though pale, was quite steady. The others were all more or less played out from the night before, and about the room were the signs of the wild frolic. A bench was upset, while broken bottles and dishes lay strewn about over a floor reeking with filth. The disgust on my face must have shown itself clearly, for it brought forth an apology from the younger Hill, who was serving up ham and eggs as best he could to the men lounging about the table.

"It's my housemaid's afternoon out," he explained with a short laugh.

"Gone for a walk in the park," added another.

"Hope Mister Connor will pardon the absence," sneered Bruce, in his most offensive manner.

"Don't mind him," said Hi under his breath, "the blue devils are runnin' him down."

This became more evident as the evening went on. From mere discourtesy Bruce passed to violence. Hi's attempts to soothe him finally drove him mad, and he drew his revolver, shouting that he could look after himself, in proof of which he began to shoot out the lights.

The men scrambled into safe corners, all but The Duke, who stood quietly by watching Bruce shoot. Then he said:

"Let me have a try, Bruce." He reached across and caught his hand.

"No! you don't," said Bruce, struggling. "No man gets my gun."

He tore madly at The Duke's hand with both of his, but in vain, calling out with angry oaths, "Let go! Let go! I'll kill you! I'll kill you!"

With a furious effort he hurled himself back from the table, dragging Duke partly across. There was a flash and a shot and Bruce collapsed, the Duke still gripping him. When they lifted him up he was found to have an ugly wound in his arm, the bullet having passed through the fleshy part. I bound it up as best I could and tried to persuade him to go lay down. But he swore he'd go home. Nothing could stop him. Finally The Duke agreed to go with him, and off they set, Bruce loudly protesting that he could get home alone and did not want anyone tagging along playing nursemaid.

It cast a dismal pall over the men and we all went home feeling rather sick. It gave me no pleasure to find Skyler waiting in my shack for my report of Bruce. It was vain for me to make light of the accident to him. So I held back nothing. His eyes were wide open with concern when I had finished.

"You needn't tell me not to worry," he said, "you are anxious yourself. I see it in your face."

"Well, there's no use trying to keep things from you," I replied, "but I am only a little anxious. Don't you go and work yourself up into a fever over it."

He would not leave till I had promised to take him up to visit Bruce the next day, though I was doubtful enough of his reception. But the following morning The Duke came down the hill, his black bronco Jingo wet with hard riding.

"Better come up, Connor," he said to me, gravely, "and bring your bromides along. Bruce has had a bad night and morning and fell asleep only before I came away. I expect he'll wake in delirium. It's the whiskey more than the bullet. Shakes, you know."

In ten minutes we three were on the trail, for Skyler, though not invited, had heard The Duke's coming and was determined to go with us.

"Oh, all right," said Duke, indifferently, "he probably won't recognize you anyway."

We rode hard for half and hour till we came within sight of Bruce's shack which was set back into a little poplar bluff.

"Hold up!" said The Duke. "Was that a shot?" We stood listening. A rifle-shot rang out, and we rode hard. Again Duke halted us, and there came from the shack the sound of singing. It was an old Scotch tune.

"The twenty-third Psalm," said Skyler, in a low voice.

We rode into the bluff, tied up our horses and crept to the back of the shack. Looking through a crack between the logs, I saw a gruesome thing. Bruce was sitting up in bed with a Winchester rifle across his knees and a belt of cartridges hanging over the post. His bandages were torn off, the blood from his wound was smeared over his bare arm and his pale, ghastly face; his eyes were wild with mad terror, and he was shouting at the top of his voice the words:

"The Lord's my shepherd, I'll not want,
He makes me down to lie
In pastures green, He leadeth me
The quiet waters by."

Nothing in my memory makes me chill like that picture—the low log shack, now in cheerless disorder; the ghastly object upon the bed in the corner, with blood-smeared face and arms and mad terror in the eyes; the awful psalm-singing, punctuated by the quick report of the deadly rifle.

For some moments we stood gazing at one another; then the Duke said, in a low fierce tone, more to himself than to us:

"This is the last. There'll be no more of this cursed folly among the boys."

I thought it a wise thing in Skyler that he answered not a word. The situation was one of extreme danger— a madman with a Winchester rifle. Something must be done and quickly.

But what? It would be death to anyone appearing at the door.

"I'll speak. You keep your eyes on him," said The Duke.

66

"Hello, Bruce! What's the row?" shouted Duke.

Instantly the singing stopped. A look of cunning delight came over his face as, without a word, he got his rifle ready, pointed at the door.

"Come in!" he yelled, after waiting for some moments. "Come in! You're the biggest of all the devils. Come on, I'll send you down where you belong. Come on, what's keeping you?"

Over the rifle-barrel his eyes gleamed with frenzied delight. We three looked at each other again in question.

"I don't relish a bullet much," I said.

"There are pleasanter things," responded The Duke, "and he is a fairly good shot."

Meantime the singing had started again, and looking through the chink, I saw that Bruce had got his eye on the stovepipe again. While I was looking, Skyler slipped away from us toward the door.

"Come back!" whispered Duke, "Don't be a fool! Come back, he'll shoot you dead!"

Skyler paid no heed, but stood waiting at the door. In a few moments Bruce blazed away again at the stovepipe. Immediately Skyler burst in, calling eagerly:

"Did you get him?"

"No!" said Bruce, disappointedly, "he dodged like the devil you know."

"I'll get him," said Skyler. "We'll smoke him out," as he proceeded to open the stove door.

"Stop!" screamed Bruce, "Don't open that door! It's full, I tell you." Skyler paused.

"Besides," went on Bruce, "smoke won't touch 'em."

"Oh, that's all right," said the Pilot coolly and with admirable quickness, "wood smoke, you know—they can't stand that."

This was apparently a new idea in demonology for Bruce, for he sank back, while Skyler lighted the fire and put on the kettle. He looked round for the coffee.

"Up there on that shelf," said Bruce, forgetting for the moment his devils, and pointing to a quaint, old-fashioned crockery filled with coffee.

Skyler took it down, turned it in his hands, and looked at Bruce.

"Old country, eh?"

"My mother's," said Bruce, soberly.

"I could have sworn it was my aunt's in Balleymena," said Skyler. "My aunt lived in a little stone cottage with roses all over the front of it." And on he went into an enthusiastic description of his early home. His voice was full of music, soft and soothing, and poor Bruce sank back and listened, the glitter fading from his eyes.

The Duke and I looked at each other.

"Not too bad, eh?" said The Duke, after a few moments' silence.

"Let's put up the horses," I suggested. "They won't want us for half an hour."

When we came in, the room had been set in order, the kettle was singing, the bedclothes straightened out, and Skyler had just finished washing the blood stains from Bruce's arms and neck.

"You're just in time," he said. "I didn't want to tackle these," pointing to the bandages. "I wasn't sure how to rewrap them."

All afternoon and into the night, Skyler soothed and tended the sick man, now singing softly to him, and again beguiling him with tales that meant nothing, but that possessed a strange power to quiet the nervous restlessness, due partly to the pain of the wounded arm and partly to the nerve-wrecking from his months of dissipation. The Duke seemed extremely uncomfortable. He spoke to Bruce once or twice, but the only answer was a groan or curse with an increase of restlessness.

"He'll have a close squeak," said The Duke. "That is

if he pulls out at all. He looks bad."

"He has not been altogether wise in his associations," Skyler said, looking straight into Duke's eyes.

"A real man ought to know himself when the pace is getting too swift," said The Duke, a little more quickly than was his habit.

"He respects you. Why didn't you help him?" Skyler's tones were stern and steady, and he never moved his eyes from the other man's face. But the only reply he got was a shrug of the shoulders.

When the gray of the next morning was coming in at the window The Duke rose up, gave himself a little shake and said, "I am not of any service here. I'll be back in the evening."

He went and stood for a few moments looking down on the hot fevered face; then, turning to me, he asked:

"What do you think, Connor?"

"Can't say. The bromide is holding him down just now. His bleeding is bad for that wound."

"Can I get anything?" I knew him well enough to recognize the anxiety under his indifferent manner.

"The Fort doctor ought to be fetched."

He nodded and went out.

"Have breakfast?" called out Skyler from the door.

"I shall get some at the Fort, thanks. They won't take any offense from me there," he said, smiling his cynical smile.

Skyler opened his eyes in surprise.

"What's that for?" he asked me.

"Well, he is a little cut up, and you rather rubbed it in you know," I said, for I thought Skyler had been a little hard.

"Did I say anything untrue?"

"Well, not untrue, perhaps; but truth is like medicine —not always pleasant to take." At this Skyler was silent till his patient needed him again.

It was a weary day. The intense pain from the wound and the high fever from the poison in his blood kept the poor fellow in delirium till evening. When The Duke rode up with the Fort doctor, Jingo appeared nearly as played out as a horse of his spirit ever allowed himself to become.

"Seventy miles," said The Duke, swinging himself off the saddle. "The doctor was ten miles out. How is he?"

I shook my head. He led his horse away to give him a rub and a feed.

Meantime the doctor, who was of the army and had seen service, was examining his patient. He grew more and more puzzled as he noted the various symptoms. Finally he said:

"What have you been doing to him? Why is he in this condition?" This fleabite of a wound doesn't account for all the damage done."

We stood like children reproved. Then The Duke said hesitatingly—

"I fear, Doctor, the life has been a little too hard for him. He had a severe nervous attack—seeing things, you know."

"What kind of things?"

"Things—you know. Things that aren't there. Snakes ...demons."

"Yes, I know," stormed the old doctor. "I know your lot well enough, with your head of cast-iron and no nerves to speak of. I know the crowd and how you lead them. Infernal fools! You'll get your turn some day. I've warned you before."

The Duke was standing in front of the doctor during this dressing down, smiling slightly. All at once the smile faded out and he pointed to the bed. Bruce was sitting up quiet and steady. He stretched out his hand to The Duke.

"Don't mind the old fool," he said, holding Duke's hand and looking up at him as fondly. "It's my own funeral...?"

He paused. "Perhaps it may be—who knows?" He went on, "—feel queer enough—but remember, Duke—it's my own fault—don't listen to those blanked fools," looking towards Skyler and the doctor. "My own fault" —his voice died down—"my own fault."

The Duke bent over him and laid him back on the pillow, saying, "Thanks, old chap, you're good stuff. I'll not forget. Just keep quiet and you'll be all right." He passed his cool, firm hand over the hot brow of the man looking up at him with love in his eyes, and in a few moments Bruce fell asleep.

The Duke lifted himself up, and facing the doctor, said in his coolest tone:

"Your words are more true than opportune, Doctor. Your patient will need all your attention. As for my morals, Mr. Skyler kindly entrusts himself with the care of them." These words he said with a bow towards the preacher.

"I wish him luck with his charge," snorted the doctor, turning again to the bed, where Bruce had already passed into delirium.

The memory of that vigil was like a horrible nightmare for months. Skyler lay on the floor and slept. The Duke rode off somewhere. The old doctor and I kept watch. All night poor Bruce raved in the wildest delirium, singing, now psalms, now songs, swearing at the cattle or his poker partners, and now and then, in quieter moments, he was back in his old home, a boy, with a boy's friends and sports. But nothing could stop the fever made so much worse by the alcohol in the poor man's system. It baffled the doctor, who, often during the night, declared that there was "no sense in a wound like that working up such a fever," adding curses upon the folly of The Duke and his Company.

"He ought to get over this," he answered impatiently, "but it seems," he added deliberately, "that he's fading."

Everything stood still for a moment.

It seemed impossible. Two days ago full of life, now on the way out. There crowded in upon me thoughts of his home; his mother, whose letters he used to show me full of anxious love; his wild life here, with all its impulses, its mistakes, its folly.

"How long will he last?" I asked, and my lips were dry and numb.

"Perhaps twenty-four hours, perhaps longer. He can't throw off the poison."

The old doctor proved a true prophet. After another day of agonized delirium, Bruce sank into a stupor which lasted through the night.

Then the change came. As the morning light began to grow at the eastern rim of the prairie and tip the far mountains in the west, Bruce opened his eyes and looked about upon us. The doctor had gone; Duke had not come back; Skyler and I were alone. He gazed at us steadily for some moments; read our faces; a look of wonder came into his eyes.

"Is it coming?" he asked in a faint, awed voice. "Do you really think I must go?"

The eager appeal in his voice and the wistful longing in the wide-open, startled eyes were too much for Skyler. He backed behind me and I could hear him weeping like a baby. Bruce heard him too.

"Is that the preacher?" he asked. Instantly Skyler pulled himself together, wiped his eyes and came round to the other side of the bed and looked down, smiling.

"Do *you* say I am dying?" The voice was strained in its earnestness. I felt a thrill of admiration go through me as our Sky Pilot answered in a clear voice: "They say so, Bruce. But you are not afraid? You've known

Him all along, haven't you?"

Bruce kept his eyes on his face and answered with grave hesitation, "No—not—afraid—but I'd like to live a little longer. I've made such a mess of it, I've failed Him so. I'd like to try again."

Then he paused and his lips quivered a little. "There's my mother, you know," he added apologetically, "and Jim, my younger brother."

"Yes, I know, Bruce, but it won't be very long for them too, and it's a good place you'll be going. A very good place."

"Yes, I believe it all—always did—talked rot though —you'll forgive me for that?" he asked, trying to raise on his elbows.

"Of course I do," said Skyler, "but don't try to raise yourself up," he added quickly, and Bruce smiled a little and closed his eyes, and lay back, saying, "I'm so tired." But he immediately opened them again and looked up.

"What is it?" asked Skyler, smiling down into his eyes.

"The Duke," the poor lips whispered.

"He is coming," said Skyler confidently, though how he knew I could not tell. But even as he spoke, looking out of the window, I saw Jingo come swinging round the bluff. Bruce heard the beat of his hoofs, smiled, opened his eyes and waited. The leap of joy in his eyes as The Duke came in, clean, cool, and fresh as the morning, went to my heart.

Neither man said a word, but Bruce took hold of The Duke's hand in both of his. He was fast growing weaker. I gave him a sip of brandy, and he recovered a little strength.

"I am dying, Duke," he said, quietly. "Promise you won't blame yourself."

"I can't promise that, old man," said The Duke, with a shudder. "Would to heaven I could."

"You were just too strong for me, and you didn't know, did you?" and the weak voice had a caress in it.

"No, no! God knows," said The Duke, hurriedly.

There was a long silence, and again Bruce opened his eyes and whispered:

"The Sky Pilot."

Skyler came to him.

"Read 'The Prodigal,' " he said faintly, and in Skyler's clear, sweet voice the music of that matchless story fell upon our ears.

When he was through, again Bruce's eyes sought me. I bent over him.

"My letter," he said, faintly, "in my coat—"

I brought to him the last letter from his mother. He held the envelope before his eyes, then handed it to me, whispering:

"Read."

I opened the letter and looked at the words, "My darling Davie."

My tongue stuck and I could not make another sound. Skyler put out his hand and took it from me. The Duke rose to go out, calling me with his eyes, but Bruce motioned him to stay, and he sat down and bowed his head, while Skyler read the letter.

His tones were clear and steady till he came to the last words, when his voice broke and ended in a sob:

"And oh, Davie, laddie, if ever your heart turns home again, remember the door is aye open, and it's joy you'll bring with you to us all."

Bruce lay quite still, and from his closed eyes big tears ran down his cheeks. It was his last farewell to her whose love had been to him the anchor to all things pure on earth, and to heaven beyond.

He took the letter from Skyler's hand, put it with difficulty to his lips, and then, touching the open Bible, he said between his breaths:

"It's—very like—there's really—no fear, is there?"

"No, no!" said Skyler, with cheerful, confident voice, though his tears were flowing. "No fear of your welcome."

His eyes met mine. I bent over him. "Tell her—" and his voice faded away.

"What shall I tell her?" I asked, trying to recall him.

But the message was never given. He moved one hand slowly toward The Duke till it touched his head. The Duke lifted his face and looked down at him, and then he did a beautiful thing. He stooped over and kissed the lips grown so white, and then the hand that still clutched the treasured letter.

The light came back into the eyes of the dying man, he smiled once more, and smilingly faced toward the Great Beyond. The morning air, fresh from the sun-tipped mountains and sweet with the scent of the June roses, came blowing soft and cool through the open window upon the dead, smiling face. And it seemed fitting so. It came from the land of the Morning.

Again The Duke did a beautiful thing; for, reaching across his dead friend, he offered his hand to the preacher. "Mr. Skyler," he said, with fine courtesy, "you are a brave man and a good man. I ask your forgiveness for much rudeness."

But Skyler only shook his head while he took the outstretched hand.

"The Company of the Noble Seven will meet no more," said The Duke.

They did meet, however, but when they did, The Pilot was in the chair, and it was not for poker.

The Pilot had got his grip on them, as Bill said.

10.
GWEN'S FIRST PRAYERS

Bruce's death was a blow to most everyone in the small community—a tragedy that for a few short days beyond the funeral caused all to realize our mortality. The Muirs mourned as deeply as any of the range men, save the Duke, whose private grief was worse than he would let anyone know.

Within a few weeks, however, though not forgotten, the death was necessarily put behind us. We were again occupied by the concerns of our daily work and routines, until such time as we would again draw together for common celebrations or calamities. The next of these latter occurrences would come to pass far sooner, and in more heart-wrenching fashion, than any of us could have anticipated.

It was with hesitation, and almost fear, that I had begun tutoring Gwen several weeks earlier. But even had I been able to foresee the endless series of exasperations through which she was to conduct me, I would still have undertaken the task. For the spunky woman-child—with all her willfulness, her tempers, and her pride—made me, as she did all others, her willing slave. And without even realizing that it was happening, she soon became the chief object of my teaching efforts.

Her lessons went on according to her sweet will. She learned to read rapidly, for she was eager to know more of that great world of which The Duke had told her such thrilling tales. Writing she abhorred. She had no one to write to. Why should she cramp her fingers over crooked little marks? But she mastered with hardly a struggle the mysteries of figures, for she would have to sell her cattle, and "dad doesn't know when they are cheating." Her ideas of education were purely utilitarian, and what did not appear immediately useful she refused to trifle with.

So all through the following long winter she tried my soul with her strong will and independent spirit. An appeal to her father did no good. She would wind her long, thin arms about his neck, and the old man was quite helpless to exert any authority. The Duke could do the most with her. To please him she would struggle with her writing for an hour at a time, but even his influence and authority had its limits.

"Must I?" she said one day, in answer to a demand of his for more faithful study; "must I?" And throwing up her proud little head, she looked straight at him from her blue-gray eyes and asked the monosyllabic question, "Why?"

The Duke looked back at her with his slight smile for a few moments, and then said in cold, even tones:

"I really don't know why," and turned his back on her.

Immediately she sprang at him, shook him by the arm, and quivering with passion, cried:

"You are not to speak to me like that, and you are not to turn your back that way!"

"What a princess you are!" he said admiringly. Then

he added, smiling sadly:

"Was I harsh, Gwen? Then I am sorry."

Her rage was gone. She was too proud to show her feelings, so she just looked at him with softening eyes, then sat down to the work she had refused.

As The Duke rode home with me that night, he said with hesitation, "She ought to have some religion, poor child. The Pilot might be of service if you could bring him up. Women need that sort of thing; it refines them, you know."

"Would she have him?" I asked.

"You might suggest it," he replied, doubtfully.

I did so, introducing somewhat clumsily The Duke's name.

"The Duke says he is to make me good?" she cried. "Then I won't have him, I hate him, and you too!"

For that day she refused all lessons, and when The Duke appeared she greeted him with the exclamation, "I won't have your old Sky Pilot—I don't want to be good, and—and—you think he's no good yourself." At this The Duke opened his eyes.

"How do you know? I never said so!"

"You laughed about him to dad one day."

"Did I?" said The Duke, gravely. "Then I hasten to assure you that I have changed my mind. He is a good, brave man."

"He falls off his horse," she said, with contempt.

"Oh, I think he can probably stay on by now," replied The Duke, repressing a smile.

"Besides," she went on, "he's just a kid; Bill said so. Anyway, he is not to come here."

But he did come. And with none other than Gwen as his escort, one threatening August evening.

"I found him in the creek," she announced, marching in with Skyler half drowned. I smiled broadly at the sight as I laid out Gwen's lessons for the next few days.

"I think I could have crossed," he said, apologetically, "My pony was about to get on his feet again."

"No, you wouldn't," she protested. "You would have been down the canyon by now, and you ought to be thankful."

"Oh, I am," he hastened to say, "very! But," he added, unwilling to give up his contention, "I have crossed the Swan before."

"Not when it was in flood."

"Yes, when it was in flood, higher than now."

"Not where the banks are rocky."

"No," he hesitated.

"There! Then you *would* have drowned but for my lariat!" she cried, triumphantly.

To this he doubtfully agreed.

They were a lot alike—high in temper, enthusiasm, vivid imagination, and sensitive feeling. When the Old Timer came in Gwen introduced Skyler as having been rescued from a watery grave by her lariat. Once and again they fought out the possibilities of drowning and escape, until Gwen almost lost her temper. She could be appeased only by the profuse expressions of gratitude on the part of Skyler for her timely assistance.

The Old Timer was perplexed. He was afraid to offend Gwen and yet unwilling to be cordial to her guest. The Pilot was quick to feel this, and soon after tea rose to go. Gwen's disappointment showed in her face.

"Ask him to stay, dad," she said in a whisper. But the half-hearted invitation acted like a spur, and Skyler was determined to leave.

"There's a bad storm coming," she said. "And besides," she added with a grin, "you can't cross the Swan —alone!" I was constrained to agree, having determined to stay the night myself. But I wisely remained silent.

Her statement settled it—the most earnest prayers of the Old Timer could not have held him back from the challenge of her voice.

We all went down to see him cross, Gwen leading her pinto. The Swan was over its banks, running swift and strong. Louis, the pony, snorted, refused, and finally plunged. Bravely he swam, till the swift-running water struck him, and over he went on his side, throwing his rider into the water. But Skyler kept his head, and holding by the stirrups, paddled along by Louis's side. When they were half way across Louis saw that he had no chance of making a landing. So, like a sensible horse, he turned back for shore. Here too the banks were high, and the pony began to grow discouraged.

"Let him float down further!" yelled Gwen. Urging her pinto along the bank, she coaxed the struggling pony down the stream until he was opposite a shelf of rock, level with the high water. Then she threw her lariat, and catching Louis around the neck and the horn of his saddle, she held tight, until, half drowned, he scrambled up the bank, dragging Skyler with him.

"There!" she said, almost victoriously, "You see, you couldn't get across!"

Skyler staggered to his feet, took a step toward her, gasped out:

"I can!" and pitched forward headlong toward the water. With a little cry she ran to him, and turned him over on his back. In a few moments he revived, sat up, and looked about.

"Where's Louis?" he said, with his face toward the swollen stream.

"Safe enough," she answered, "but you must come in, the rain is going to pour."

"No, I'm going across, " he insisted, rising.

"But your poor horse," she said, "he is tired out."

The Old Timer now joined earnestly in urging him to stay till the storm was past. Finally, with a last look at the stream, Skyler turned toward the house.

Of course I knew what would happen. Before the evening was over he had captured the household. The moment he appeared with dry clothes on, he sat down at the organ which had stood for ten years closed and silent, opened it, and began to play. As he played and sang song after song, The Old Timer's eyes began to glisten under his shaggy brows. But when he dropped into the exquisite Irish melody, "Oft in the Stilly Night," the old man drew a hard breath and groaned out to me, "It was her mother's song."

And from that time Skyler had him fast. It was easy to pass to the old hymn, "Nearer, My God, to Thee," and then The Pilot said simply, "May we have prayers?"

He looked at Gwen, but she gazed blankly at him and then at her father.

"What does he mean, dad?"

It was pitiful to see the old man's face grow slowly red under the deep tan, as he said:

"You may, sir. There's been none here for many years, and the worse for us."

He rose slowly, went into the inner room and returned with a Bible.

"It's her mother's," he said in a voice deep with emotion. "I put it in her trunk the day I laid her out yonder under the pines."

Skyler, without looking at him, rose and reverently took the book in both his hands and said gently:

"It was a hard day for you, but for her it was a door to a better life." He paused. "You did not grudge it to her?" he asked after a moment.

"Not now. But then, yes! I wanted her, we needed her." The Old Timer's tears were flowing.

Skyler put his hand tenderly upon the old man's shoulder as if he had been his father. Then he said in his clear voice, "Some day you will go through that door—to her."

Gwen gazed at all this with eyes wide open in amazement. She had never seen her father weep since the awful day she could never forget, when he had knelt in dumb agony beside the bed on which her mother lay white and still. Nor would he heed her, till, climbing up, she tried to make her mother waken and hear her cries. Then he had caught her up in his arms, pressing her with tears and great sobs to his heart.

Tonight she seemed to feel again that something was wrong. She went and stood by her father, and stroking his gray hair kindly, she said, "What is he saying, daddy? Is he making you cry?"

"No, no, child," said the old man hastily. "Sit here and listen."

Then while the storm raged outside, we three sat listening to that ancient gospel story of love. And as the words fell like sweet music upon our ears, the old man sat with eyes that looked far away, while the child listened with devouring eagerness.

"Is it a fairy tale, daddy?" she asked when Skyler paused. "It isn't true, is it?" Her voice had a pleading note difficult for the old man to bear.

"Yes, yes, my child," he said brokenly. "God forgive me!"

"Of course it's true," said Skyler quickly. "I'll read it all to you tomorrow. It's a beautiful story!"

"No," she said, with a strange curiosity. "Tonight. Read it now! Go on!" she said.

Skyler gazed at her in surprise. Then, turning to the old man, he said:

"Shall I?"

The Old Timer simply nodded, and the reading went on.

Those had not been my most religious days and the faith of my childhood was not as it had been. But as Skyler carried us through those matchless scenes of self-forgetting love and service, the wonder in the child's face as she listened, the appeal in her voice as, now to her father, then to me, she cried, "Is *that* true, too? Is it *all* true?" made it impossible for me to hesitate in my answer.

I was glad to find it easy to give my firm agreement to the truth of that tale of wonder. As more and more it dawned upon Skyler that the story he was reading, so old to him, was new to one in that listening group, his face began to glow and his eyes to blaze. He saw and showed me things that night I had never seen before. Nor have I seen them since. The great figure of the Gospels lived, moved before our eyes. We saw Him bend to touch the blind, we heard Him speak His marvelous teaching, we felt the throbbing excitement of the crowds that pressed against Him.

Suddenly Skyler stopped, turned over the leaves, and began again, "And He led them out as far as to Bethany. And He lifted up His hands and blessed them. And it came to pass as He blessed them He was parted from them and a cloud received Him out of their sight."

There was silence for some minutes. Then Gwen said:

"Where did He go?"

"Up into Heaven," answered Skyler, simply.

"That's where mother is," she said to her father, who nodded in reply.

"Does He know?" she asked. The old man looked distressed.

"Of course He does," said Skyler, "and she sees Him all the time."

"Oh, daddy!" she cried, "isn't that good?"

But the old man only hid his face in his hands.

"Yes," went on Skyler, "and He sees us too, and hears us speak, and knows our thoughts.

Again the look of wonder and fear came into her eyes. But she said no word. The experiences of the evening had made the world new for Gwen. It could never be the same to her again. It gave me an odd feeling to see her, when we three knelt to pray, standing helplessly looking on not knowing what to do. Then she sank beside her father, and winding her arms about his neck, clung to him as the words of prayer were spoken into the ear of Him whom no man can see, but who we believe is near to all that call upon Him.

I could only marvel at the impact of The Pilot on those lives he touched, first to have heard the beauty of dear Bruce's final prayers, and now these, Gwen's first "prayers." In them Gwen's part was small, for fear and wonder filled her heart. But the day was to come, and all too soon, when she should have to pour out her soul with strong crying and tears.

11.
GWEN'S CHALLENGE

Gwen was certainly wild and willful as Skyler said. Even Bronco Bill and Hi Kendall would say so, without, of course, lessening one bit of their admiration for her. For all her sixteen years she had lived chiefly with wild things. The cattle on the range, wild as deer, the coyotes, the jackrabbits, and the timber wolves were her friends and teachers. The rolling prairie of the Foothill country was her home. She loved it and all things that moved upon it with passionate love, the only kind she was capable of. All summer long she spent her days riding up and down the range alone, or with her father, or with Joe, or best of all with The Duke, her hero and her friend. So she grew up strong, wholesome, and self-reliant, fearing nothing alive and as untamed as a yearling range colt.

Gwen was not beautiful. The winds and sun had left her no complexion to speak of, but the glory of her red hair, gold-red, with purple sheen, nothing could tarnish. Her eyes too, deep blue with rims of gray that flashed with the glint of steel or shone with melting light as of the stars, according to her mood—those Irish, warm, deep eyes of hers were worth a man's looking.

Of course everyone spoiled her. Ponka and her son Joe adored her, while her father and all who came within touch of her simply did whatever they thought she wanted. Even The Duke, who loved her better than anything else, offered lazy, admiring homage to his Little Princess. And certainly, when she stood straight up with her proud little gold-crowned head thrown back, flashing forth wrath or issuing imperious commands, she looked every bit a princess.

It was a great day and good day for her when she fished Skyler out of the Swan and brought him home. And the night of Gwen's first prayers, when she heard the story of the Man of Nazareth for the first time, was the best of all her nights. All through the winter, under Skyler's guidance, she with her father listening nearby, went over and over that story so old now to man, but ever becoming new, till a whole new world of mysterious Powers and Presences lay open to her imagination and became the home of great realities. She was rich in imagination and, when Skyler read Bunyan's immortal story, her mother's old copy of "Pilgrim's Progress," she moved and lived beside the pilgrim of that tale.

The Pilot himself was a new and wholesome experience to her as well. He was the first thing she had yet encountered that refused submission, and the first human being that had failed to fall down and worship her. There was something in him that would not *always* yield, and indeed, her pride and her imperious tempers he met with surprise and sometimes even with pity. This did not always please her. Occasionally she lashed out angrily against him.

One of these outbursts is stamped upon my mind, not only because of its unusual violence, but also because of the events which followed. The original cause of her rage was some trifling misdeed done her by Joe, but when I came upon the scene it was Skyler who was occupying her attention. The expression on her face appeared to stir him up.

"How dare you look at me like that?" she cried.

"How very extraordinary that you can't keep hold of yourself better!" he answered.

"I can!" she stamped, "And I shall do as I like!"

"It is a great pity," he said, with provoking calm. "Besides, it is weak and silly." His words were unfortunate if he thought to settle her down.

"Weak!" she gasped, when her breath came back to her. "Weak!"

"Yes," he said, "very weak and childish."

When she had recovered a little from the force of his words, she cried vehemently:

"I'm not weak! I'm strong! I'm stronger than you are! I'm strong as—as—a man!"

Skyler ignored her and went on.

"In many ways you are strong, Gwen," he said. "But not in the way that takes the greatest kind of strength of all—controlling yourself. You're not strong enough to keep your temper down."

And then, as she had no reply ready, he continued. "And really, Gwen, it is not right. You must not go on in this way."

Again his words were unfortunate.

"*Must not!*" she cried, adding an inch to her height. "Who says so?"

She was greatly taken back, and gave a quick glance over her shoulder as if to see Him, who would dare to say *must not* to her; but, recovering, she answered sullenly:

"I don't care!"

"Don't care for God?" Skyler's voice was quiet and solemn, but something in his manner angered her more and she blazed forth again.

"I don't care for anyone, and I *shall* do as I please."

Skyler looked at her sadly for a moment, and then said slowly, "Someday, Gwen, you will not be able to do as you like."

I well remember the settled defiance in her tone and manner as she took a step nearer him and answered in a voice trembling with anger—

"Listen! I have always done as I like, and I shall do as I like till I die!"

She rushed out of the house and down toward the canyon, her refuge from all disturbing things, and especially from herself.

I could not shake the impression her words made upon me. "That sounds uncommonly like a challenge to the Almighty," I said to Skyler, as we rode away.

Within only a week her challenge was accepted, and how fiercely and how gallantly did she struggle against it.

It was The Duke who brought me the news, and as he told me the story his self-command was gone. For in the gloom of the canyon where he overtook me I could see that his face was ghastly white, and even his iron nerve could not keep the tremor from his voice.

"I've just sent up the doctor," was his answer to my greeting. "I looked for you last night, couldn't find you, and so rode off to the Fort."

"What's up?" I said with fear in my heart, for no little thing moved The Duke.

"Haven't you heard? It's Gwen," he said.

On her father's buckskin bronco she had gone with The Duke to the big plain above the cut-bank where Joe was herding the cattle. The day was hot and a storm was in the air. They found Joe riding up and down, singing to keep the cattle quiet, but having a hard time holding the bunch from breaking.

While The Duke was riding around the far side of

the herd, a cry from Gwen arrested his attention. Joe was in trouble. His horse, a half-broken cayuse, had stumbled into a badger-hole and had bolted, leaving Joe on the ground to the mercy of the cattle.

At once they began to sniff suspiciously at this phenomenon, a man on foot, and to follow cautiously on his track. Joe kept his head and walked slowly out, till all at once a young cow began to bawl and to paw the ground. In another minute one, and then another, of the cattle began to toss their heads and bunch and bellow till the whole herd of two hundred were after Joe. Then Joe lost his head and ran. Immediately the whole herd broke into a thundering gallop with heads and tails aloft and horns rattling like the loading of a regiment of rifles.

"Two more minutes," said The Duke, "would have done Joe in, for I could never have reached him. But in spite of my most frantic warnings and signalings, right into the face of that mad, bellowing, thundering mass of steers rode that little girl. Nerve! I have some myself, but I couldn't have done it. She swung her horse round Joe and sailed out with him, with the herd bellowing at the tail of her bronco. I've seen some courageous things in my day, but for sheer cool bravery, nothing touches that."

"How did it end? Did they run them down?" I asked with fear in my voice.

"No, they crowded her toward the cut-bank. She was edging them off and was almost past, when they came to a place where the bank bit in, and her iron-mouthed brute wouldn't swerve but went pounding on, broke through, and plunged. She couldn't spring free because of Joe, and pitched headlong over the bank, while the cattle went thundering past. I flung myself off Jingo and slid down somehow into the sand, thirty feet below. There was Joe safe enough, but the bronco lay with a broken leg, and half under him was Gwen. She hardly knew she was hurt, but waved her hand to me and cried, 'Wasn't that a race? I couldn't swing this hard-headed brute. Get me out.' But even as she spoke the light faded from her eyes, she stretched out her hands to me, saying faintly, 'Oh, Duke,' and lay back white and still. We put a bullet into the buckskin's head, and carried her home in our jackets, and there she lies without a sound from her poor white lips."

The Duke was badly broken up. I had never seen him show such grief before, even for Bruce, but as he finished the story he stood ghastly and shaking. He read my surprise in my face and said:

"Look here, old chap, don't think me quite a fool. You can't know what that little girl has done for me all these years. Her trust in me—it is extraordinary how utterly she trusts me—somehow held me up to my best. It is the one bright spot in my life in this blessed country."

Then after a pause, he added, "If Gwen goes, I must pull out. I could not stand it."

As we rode up to the cabin, the doctor walked out.

"Well, what do you think?" asked The Duke.

"Can't say yet," replied the old man, gruff with long army practice, "bad enough. Good night."

But The Duke's hand fell upon his shoulder with a grip that must have gone to the bone, and in a husky voice he asked, "Will she live?"

The doctor squirmed but could not shake off that crushing grip.

"Let go! you young tiger. What do you think I am made of?" he cried angrily. "I didn't suppose I was coming to a bear's den, or I should have brought a gun."

It was only by the most complete apology that The Duke could mollify the old doctor sufficiently to get his opinion.

"No, she will not die! Great bit of stuff, that girl!

Better she should die, perhaps! But can't say yet for two weeks. Now remember," he added sharply, looking into The Duke's face, "her spirits must be kept up. I have lied most fully and cheerfully to them inside; you must do the same."

Then the doctor strode away, calling out:

"Joe! Here, Joe! Where is he gone? Joe, I say! Extraordinary selection providence makes at times; we could have spared that lazy scion with pleasure! Joe! Oh, here you are! Where in thunder—" But here the doctor stopped abruptly. The agony in the dark face before him was too much even for the gruff doctor. Straight and stiff Joe stood by the horse's head till the doctor had mounted, then with great effort he said:

"Little miss, she go dead?"

"Dead!" called out the doctor, glancing at the open window. "Why, bless your old copper carcass, no! Gwen will show you yet how to rope a steer."

Joe took a step nearer, and lowering his tone said:

"You speak me true? Me man, me no papoose." The piercing black eyes searched the doctor's face. The doctor hesitated a moment, and then with an air of great candor, said cheerily:

"That's all right, Joe. Miss Gwen will cut circles round your old cayuse yet. But remember," and the doctor was very impressive, "you must make her laugh everyday."

Joe folded his arms across his breast and stood like a statue till the doctor rode away. Then to us he grunted out:

"Him good man, eh?"

"Good man," answered The Duke, adding, "but remember, Joe, what he told you to do. Must make her laugh everyday."

Poor Joe! Humor was not his trade and his attempts in that direction in the weeks that followed would have been humorous were they not so pathetic. How I did my part I cannot tell. Those weeks are to me now like the memory of an ugly nightmare. The ghostly old man moving out and in of his little daughter's room in useless, dumb agony; Ponka's woe-stricken Indian face; Joe's extraordinary and unusual but loyal attempts at fun-making grotesquely sad, and The Duke's unvarying and invincible cheeriness. These furnish light and shade for the picture my memory brings me of Gwen in those days.

For the first two weeks she was simply heroic. She bore her pain without a groan, submitted to the imprisonment which was the hardest part, with patience. Joe, Duke, and I carried out our instructions exactly to the letter. She never doubted, and we never let her doubt but that in a few weeks she would be on the pinto's back again and after the cattle. She made us pass our word for this till it seemed as if she must have read the falsehoods on our brows.

"To lie cheerfully with her eyes upon my face calls for more than I possess," said The Duke one day. "The doctor should supply us tonics. It is an arduous task."

She believed us absolutely, and made plans for the fall "roundup," and for hunts and rides till one's heart grew sick. As to the ethical problem involved, I decline to express an opinion, but we had no need to wait for our punishment. Her trust in us, her eager and confident expectation of the return of her happy, free, outdoor life; these brought to us who knew how vain they were, their own adequate punishment for every false assurance we gave. How bright and brave she was those first days! How resolute to get back to the world of air and light outside!

But she would need all her brightness and courage and resolution before she would be done with her long fight.

12.
GWEN'S CANYON

Gwen's hope and bright courage, in spite of her pain, were wonderful to witness. But all this cheery hope was finally snuffed out as a candle, leaving darkness to settle down in that sickroom from the day of the doctor's next consultation.

The verdict was clear and final. The old doctor, who loved Gwen as his own, was inclined to hope against hope, but Fawcett, the clever young doctor from the distant town, was positive in his opinion.

The scene is still clear to me now after many years. We three stood in the outer room; The Duke and her father were with Gwen. So earnest was the discussion that none of us heard the door open just as young Fawcett was saying in incisive tones:

"No! I can see no hope. She can never walk again."

There was a cry behind us.

"What! Never walk again! It's a lie!" There stood the Old Timer, white, fierce, and shaking.

"Hush!" said the old doctor, pointing at the open door. But he was too late. Even as he spoke, there came from the inner room a wild, unearthly cry as of some dying thing and, as we stood gazing at one another with awe-striken faces, we heard Gwen's voice in pain.

"Daddy! Daddy! Come back! What do they say? Tell me, daddy. It is not true! It is not true! Look at me, daddy!"

She pulled at her father's haggard face from the bed.

"Oh, daddy, daddy, you know it's true. Never walk again!"

She turned with a pitiful cry to The Duke, who stood white and stiff with arms drawn tight across his breast on the other side of the bed.

"Oh, Duke, did you hear them? You told me to be brave, and I tried not to cry when they hurt me. But I can't be brave now! Can I, Duke? Oh, Duke! Never to ride again!"

She stretched out her hands to him. But The Duke, leaning over her and holding her hand fast in his, could only say brokenly over and over, "Don't, Gwen! Don't, Gwen, dear!"

But the pitiful pleading voice went on.

"Oh, Duke! Must I always lie here? Must I? Why must I?"

"God knows," answered The Duke under his breath. "I don't!"

She caught at the word.

"Does He?" she cried eagerly. Then she paused suddenly, turned to me and said, "Do you remember the preacher said some day I could not do as I liked?"

I was puzzled.

"The Sky Pilot," she cried impatiently. "Don't you remember? And I said I should do as I liked till I died."

I nodded and said, "But you know you didn't mean it."

94

"But I did, and I do," she cried, with passionate vehemence, "and I will do as I like! I will not lie here! I will ride! I will! I will! I will!" She struggled up, clenched her fists, then sank back faint and weak. It was not a pleasant sight. Her rage against God was so defiant and so helpless.

The following were dreadful weeks for Gwen and for all near her. The constant pain could not break her proud spirit. She shed no tears, but she fretted and chafed and grew more demanding every day. She drove Ponka and Joe like a slave master, and even her father, when he could not understand her wishes, she impatiently banished from her room. Only The Duke could please or bring her any cheer, and even he began to feel that the day was not far off when he too would fail. The very thought made him despair. Her pain was hard to bear, but harder than that was her longing for the open air and the free, flower-strewn, breeze-swept prairie. Yet most pitiful of all were the days when, in her utter weariness and uncontrollable unrest, she would pray to be taken down into the canyon.

"Oh, it is so cool and shady," she would plead, "and the flowers up in the rocks and the vines and things are all so lovely. I am always better there. I know I should be better," till The Duke would be distracted and would come to me and wonder what the end of it all would be.

One day, when the strain had been worse than usual, The Duke rode down to me and said, "Look here, this thing can't go on. Where is Skyler? Why doesn't he stay around instead of traveling all around through the hills."

"He's gone where he was sent," I replied shortly. "And besides, you don't set much store by him when he does come round. In any case, he is gone on a trip through the Dog Lake country. He'll be back by the end of next week."

"Well, bring him up here," said The Duke, "he may be of some use. Anyway it will be a new face for her, poor child." Then he added, rather penitently, "I fear this thing is getting to my nerves. She almost drove me out today. Don't lay it up against me, old chap."

It was a new thing to hear The Duke confess his need of any man, much less penitence for a fault. I felt my eyes growing dim, but I replied, "I'll bring Skyler up when he gets back."

It was amazing how we had all come to confide in Skyler during his year of missionary work among us. Somehow the name of "Sky Pilot" seemed to express better than anything else the place he held with us. Certain it is that when, in their dark hours, any of the fellows felt in need of help to strike the "upward trail," they went to The Pilot whom they felt knew the way better than anyone else in those parts. And so the name first given in derision came to be the name that expressed most truly the deep and tender feeling these rough, big-hearted men had for him.

When The Pilot came home I carefully prepared him for his trial, telling all that Gwen had suffered, trying to make him feel how desperate was her condition when even The Duke had to confess himself beaten. He did not seem sufficiently impressed. Then I told him of her fierce willfulness and her impatience with those who loved her and were wearing out their souls and bodies for her. "In short," I concluded, "she doesn't care a thing for anyone but herself, and will yield to neither man nor God."

Skyler's eyes had been kindling as I talked, but he only answered quietly:

"What could you expect?"

"Well, I do think she might show some signs of gratitude and some gentleness towards those ready to die for her."

"Oh, you do?" he said. "You all combine to ruin her

96

temper and disposition with foolish flattery and weak yielding to her whims, right or wrong. You smile at her imperious pride and encourage her willfulness, and then you wonder at the results. Oh, you are a fine lot, The Duke and all of you!"

He had a most exasperating way of putting one in the wrong. I wondered what The Duke would say to this notion. All the following day, which was Sunday, I could see that Gwen was on Skyler's mind. He was struggling with the age old problem of pain.

Monday morning found us on the way to the Old Timer's ranch. And what a morning it was! How beautiful our world seemed! About us rolled the round-topped, velvet hills, brown and yellow or faintly green, spreading out behind us to the broad prairie, and before, clambering up and up to meet the purple bases of the great mountains that lay their mighty length along the horizon and thrust up white, sunlit peaks into the blue sky. On the hillsides and down in the sheltering hollows we could see groups of cattle and horses feeding upon the rich grasses. High above, the sky, cloudless and blue, arched its great kindly roof from prairie to mountain peaks. And over all, above, below, upon prairie, hillsides and mountains, the sun poured its floods of radiant yellow light.

As we followed the trail that wound up and into the heart of these rounded hills and ever nearer to the purple mountains, the morning breeze swept down to meet us, bearing a thousand scents, and filling us with its own fresh life. One can know the quickening joyousness of these Foothill breezes only after he has drunk with wide-open mouth, deep and full of them.

Through all this mingling beauty of sunlit hills and shady hollows and purple snow-peaked mountains, we rode with hardly a word, every minute adding to our heart-filling delight, but ever with the thought of the little room where, shut in from all this outside glory, lay Gwen, heart-sore with anger and longing. This must have been in Skyler's mind, for he suddenly held up his horse and burst out:

"Poor Gwen, how she loves all this! —it is her very life. How can she help fretting the heart out of her? To see this no more!" He flung himself off his bronco and said, as if thinking aloud, "It is too awful! God help me, what can I say to her?"

He threw himself down upon the grass and turned over on his face. After a few minutes he appealed to me, and his face was sorely troubled.

"How can I go to her? It seems to me sheerest mockery to speak of patience and submission to a wild young thing from whom all this is suddenly snatched forever."

Then he slowly remounted and we rode hard for another hour, till we came to the mouth of the canyon. Here the trail grew difficult and we slowed to a walk. As we went down into the cool depths, the spirit of the canyon came to meet us and took The Pilot in its grip. He rode in front, feasting his eyes on all the wonders in that storehouse of beauty. Trees of many kinds deepened the shadows of the canyon. Over us waved the big elms that grew up here and there out of the bottom, and around their feet clustered low cedars, hemlocks and balsams, while the sturdy, rugged oaks and delicate trembling poplars clung to the rocky sides and clambered up and out to the canyon's sunny lips. Back of all, the great black rocks, decked with mossy bits and clinging things, glistened cool and moist between the parting trees. From many a cozy nook the dainty clematis and columbine shook out their bells, and lower down, from beds of many-colored moss the late wind-flower and maidenhair and tiny violet lifted up brave, sweet faces.

Through the canyon the Little Swan sang its song to rocks and flowers and overhanging trees, a song of many tones, deep-booming where it took its first sheer plunge, gay-chattering where it threw itself down the ragged rocks, and soft-murmuring where it lingered about the roots of the loving, listening elms.

A cool, sweet, soothing place it was, with all its shades and sounds and silences. And lest it should be sad to any, the sharp, quick sunbeams danced and laughed down through all its leaves upon mosses, flowers and rocks. No wonder that Skyler, drawing a deep breath as he touched the prairie sod again, said:

"That does me good. It is better at times even than the sunny hills. This canyon is Gwen's favorite spot."

I saw that the canyon had done its work on him. His face was strong and calm as the hills on a summer morning. And with this face minutes later he came to look in on Gwen. It was one of her bad moods, but he came into the room like a summer breeze.

"Oh, Gwen!" he cried, without a word of greeting, much less of commiseration, "we have had such a ride!" And he proceeded to spread out the sunlit, round-topped hills before her imaginative mind till I could feel their very breezes in my face. The Duke had never dared such a thing. But as Skyler spoke, before she knew it, Gwen was out again upon her beloved hills, breathing their fresh, sunny air, filling her heart with their delights, till her eyes grew bright and she forgot her pain. Then, before she could remember, he had her down into the canyon, feasting her heart with its airs and sights and sounds. The black, glistening rocks, trickling out with moss and trailing vines, the great elms and low green cedars, the oaks and shivering poplars, the clematis and columbine hanging from the rocky nooks, and the violets and maiden hair deep bedded in their mosses.

All this and far more he showed her with a touch so light as not to shake the morning dew from bell or leaf or frond, and with a voice so soft and full of music as to fill our hearts with the canyon's mingling sounds. As poor Gwen listened, the rapture of it drew big tears down her cheeks—alas! No longer brown, but white.

And for that day at least the dull, dead weariness was lifted from her heart.

13.
THE CANYON FLOWERS

Tom Skyler's first visit to Gwen had been a triumph. But none knew better than he that the fight was still to come, for deep in Gwen's heart were thoughts whose wounds made her forget even her physical pain.

"Was it God who let me fall?" she asked abruptly one day, and Skyler knew the fight was on. But he only answered, looking fearlessly into her eyes:

"Yes, Gwen dear."

"Why did He let me fall?" Her voice was very deliberate.

"I don't know, Gwen dear," said Skyler steadily. "Only He knows the answer to that."

"And does He know I shall never ride again? Does He know how long the days are, and the nights when I can't sleep? Does He really know?"

"Yes, Gwen dear," said Skyler, and the tears were standing in his eyes, though his voice was still steady enough.

"Are you sure he knows?" The voice was painfully intense.

"Listen to me, Gwen," began Skyler, but she cut him short.

"Are you quite sure He knows? Answer me!" she cried, with her old imperiousness.

"Yes, Gwen, He knows all about you."

"Then what do you think of Him, just because He's big and strong, treating a little girl that way?" Then she added viciously, "I hate Him! I don't care! I hate Him!"

But Skyler did not wince. I wondered how he would solve that problem which puzzled, not only Gwen, but her father, The Duke, and all of us—the *why* of human pain.

"Gwen," said Skyler, as if changing the subject, "did it hurt to put on the plaster jacket?"

"Yes!" she replied. "It was worse than anything! They had to straighten me out, you know." She shuddered at the memory of that pain.

"What a pity your father or The Duke was not here!" said Skyler, earnestly.

"Why, they were both here!"

"What a cruel shame!" burst out the preacher. "Don't they care for you any more?"

"Of course they do," said Gwen indignantly.

"Why didn't they stop the doctors from hurting you so terribly?"

"Why, they let the doctors. It's going to help me to sit up and perhaps to walk about a little," answered Gwen, with blue-gray eyes open wide.

"Oh, but..." said Skyler, "it was very mean to stand by and see you hurt like that."

"Why, you silly," replied Gwen impatiently, "they want my back to get straight and strong."

"Oh, then they didn't do it just for fun...or for nothing?" said The Pilot innocently.

Gwen gazed at him in speechless anger. Then he went on:

"Do you mean they love you though they let you be hurt; or rather they let the doctors hurt you *because* they loved you and wanted to make you better?"

Gwen kept her eyes fixed with curious earnestness upon his face till the light began to dawn.

"Do you mean," she began slowly, "that though God let me fall, He loved me?"

Skyler nodded. He could not trust his voice.

"I wonder if that can be true," she said, as if to herself.

Skyler said no more. It was enough for one day. Soon we said goodbye and came away—Skyler limp and voiceless, but I was encouraged, for I began to see a little light for Gwen.

But the fight was by no means over; indeed, it had only just begun. For when the autumn came, with its misty, purple days, most glorious of all days in the cattle country, the old restlessness came back, and with it the fierce refusal to accept her lot.

Then came the day of the roundup. Why should she have to stay while everyone else went after the cattle? The Duke would have remained with her, but she impatiently sent him away. She was weary and heartsick, and worst of all she began to feel that most terrible of burdens, the burden of her life to others. I was much relieved when Skyler came in fresh and bright, waving a bunch of wildflowers in his hand.

"I thought they were all gone," he cried. "Where do you think I found them? Right down by the big elm root!" And though he saw by the settled gloom on her face that the storm was coming, he went bravely on picturing the canyon in all the splendor of its autumn dress.

But the spell would not work. Her heart was out on the sloping hills, where the cattle were bunching and crowding with tossing heads and rattling horns, and it was in a voice very bitter and impatient that she cried:

"Oh, I am sick of all this! I want to ride! I want to see the cattle and the men and—and—and all the things outside." Skyler was cowboy enough to know the longing that tugged at her heart for one wild race after the calves or steers. But he could only say:

"Try to be patient, Gwen."

"I am patient; at least I have been patient for two whole months, and it's no use, and I don't believe God cares one bit!"

"Yes, He does, Gwen, more than any of us," replied The Pilot earnestly.

"No, He does not care," she answered with angry emphasis. Skyler made no reply.

"Perhaps," she went on, "He's angry because I said I didn't care for Him, do you remember? That was very bad of me. But don't you think I've been punished enough now? You made me very angry, and I didn't really mean it."

Poor Gwen! God had grown to be very real to her during these weeks of pain, and very terrible. The minister looked down a moment into the blue-gray eyes, grown so big and so pitiful, and hurriedly dropping on his knees beside the bed, he said, in a very unsteady voice:

"Oh, Gwen, Gwen, He's not like that. Don't you remember how Jesus was with the poor sick people? That's what He's like."

"Could Jesus make me well?"

"Yes, Gwen."

"Then why doesn't He?" she asked. There was no impatience now, only trembling anxiety as she went on in a timid voice, "I asked Him to, over and over, and said I would wait two months, and now it's more than three. Are you quite sure He hears?"

She raised herself on her elbow and gazed searchingly into Skyler's face. I was glad it was not into mine. As she uttered the words, "Are you quite sure?" one felt that things were in the balance. I could not help looking at the preacher anxiously. What would he answer?

Skyler gazed out of the window upon the hills for a few moments. How long the silence seemed! Then, turning, he looked into the eyes that searched his so steadily and answered simply:

"Yes, Gwen, I am quite sure!" Then, he got her mother's Bible and said, "Now, Gwen, try to see it as I read." But, before he read, with the true artist's instinct he created the proper atmosphere. By a few vivid words he made us feel the pathetic loneliness of the Man of Sorrows in His last sad days. Then he read that masterpiece of all tragedy, the story of Gethsemane. And as he read we saw it all. The garden and the trees and the sorrow-stricken Man alone with His mysterious agony. We heard the prayer so submissive and then, for answer, the crowd and the traitor.

Gwen was far too quick to need explanation, and Skyler only said, "You see, Gwen, God gave nothing but the best—to His own Son only the best."

"The best? They took Him away, didn't they?" She knew the story well.

"Yes, but listen."

He turned the leaves rapidly and read, " 'We see Jesus for the suffering of death crowned with glory and honor.' That is how He got His Kingdom."

Gwen listened silent but unconvinced, then said slowly:

"But how can this be best for me? I am no use to anyone. It can't be best to just lie here and make them all wait on me, and—and—I did want to help daddy—and—oh—I know they will get tired of me! They are getting tired already—I—I—can't help being hateful."

By this time she was sobbing as I had never heard before—deep, passionate sobs.

Then again The Pilot had an inspiration.

"Now, Gwen," he said severely, "you know we're not as mean as that, and that you're just talking nonsense. So I'm going to smooth out your red hair and tell you a story."

"It's *not* red," she cried between her sobs.

"It is red, as red can be; a beautiful, shining purple *red*," said The Pilot emphatically, beginning to brush.

"Purple!" cried Gwen scornfully.

"Yes, I've seen it in the sun, purple. Haven't you?" said The Pilot, appealing to me. "My story is about the canyon," he went on, "our canyon, your canyon, down there."

"Is it true?" asked Gwen, already soothed by the cool, quick-moving hands.

"True? It's as true as—as—" he glanced round the room, "as the Pilgrim's Progress." This was satisfactory, and the story went on.

"At first there were no canyons, but only the broad, open prairie. One day the Master of the Prairie, walking out over his great lawns where there were only grasses, asked the Prairie, 'Where are your flowers?' And the Prairie said, 'Master, I have no seeds.' Then he spoke to the birds, and they carried seeds of every kind of flower and strewed them far and wide. And soon the Prairie bloomed with crocuses and roses and buffalo beans and the yellow crowfoot and the wild sunflowers and the red lilies all the summer long.

"Then the Master came and was well pleased. But he missed the flowers he loved best of all, and he said to the Prairie, 'Where are the clematis and the columbine, the sweet violets and wind flowers, and all the ferns and flowering shrubs?' Again he spoke to the birds, and again they carried all the seeds and strewed them far and wide.

"But again when the Master came he could not find

the flowers he loved best of all. So he said, 'Where are those, my sweetest flowers?' and the Prairie cried sorrowfully, 'Oh, Master, I cannot keep the flowers, for the winds sweep fiercely and the sun beats upon my breast, and they wither up and fly away.' Then the Master spoke to the Lightning, and with one swift flow the Lightning cleft the Prairie to the heart. And the Prairie rocked and groaned in agony, and for many a day moaned bitterly over its black, jagged, gaping wound. But the Little Swan poured its waters through the cleft, and carried down deep black mould, and once more the birds carried seeds and strewed them in the canyon. And after a long time the rough rocks were decked out with soft mosses and trailing vines, and all the nooks were hung with clematis and columbine, and great elms lifted their huge tops high up into the sunlight, and down about their feet clustered the low cedars and balsams, and everywhere the violets and wind-flower and maidenhair grew and bloomed, till the canyon, the deep canyon, became the Master's place for rest and peace and joy."

The tale was ended, and Gwen lay quiet for some moments, then said gently, "Yes! The canyon flowers are the best. Tell me what it means."

Then The Pilot read to her, "The fruits—I'll read 'flowers'—of the Spirit are love, joy, peace, long-suffering, gentleness, goodness, faith, meekness, self-control, and some of these grow only in the canyon."

"Which are the canyon flowers? asked Gwen softly.

Skyler answered, "Gentleness, meekness, self-control, But though the others—love, joy, peace—bloom in the open, yet never with so rich a bloom and so sweet a perfume as in the canyon."

For a long time Gwen lay quite still, and then said wistfully, while her lip trembled, "There are no flowers in my canyon, only ragged rocks."

"Some day they will bloom, Gwen dear. He will find

them and we too shall see them."

Then he said goodbye and took me away. He had done his work that day.

We rode through the big gate, down the sloping hill, past the smiling, twinkling little lake, and down again out of the broad sunshine into the shadows and soft lights of the canyon. As we followed the trail that wound among the elms and cedars, the very air was full of gentle stillness. And as we moved we seemed to feel the touch of loving hands that lingered while they left us, and every flower and tree and vine and shrub and the soft mosses and the deep-bedded ferns whispered, as we passed, of love and peace and joy.

To The Duke it was all a wonder, for as the days shortened outside they brightened inside. And every day, more and more Gwen's room became the brightest spot in all the house. Finally he asked Skyler:

"What did you do to the Little Princess, and what's all this about the canyon and its flowers?"

Skyler said, looking wistfully into The Duke's eyes:

"The fruits of the Spirit are love, peace, long-suffering, gentleness, goodness, faith, meekness, self-control, and some of these are found only in the canyon."

Then The Duke stood up straight, handsome and strong, looked back at The Pilot and said, putting out his hand:

"Do you know, I believe you're right."

"Yes, I'm quite sure," answered Skyler simply. Then, holding The Duke's hand as long as one man dare hold another's, he added, "When you come to your own canyon...remember."

"When I come?" said The Duke, and a quick spasm of pain passed over his handsome face—"God help me, it's not too far away now." Then he smiled again, his old smile, and said:

"Yes, you are all right, for of all flowers I have seen, none are fairer or sweeter than those that are waving in Gwen's Canyon."

14.
BILL'S BLUFF

Skyler had long set his heart on the building of a church in the Swan Creek district, partly because he was human and wished to set a mark of remembrance upon the country, but more because he held the sensible opinion that a congregation, like a man, must have a home if it is to stay.

All through the summer he kept setting this as an object at once desirable and possible to achieve. But few agreed with him.

Little Mrs. Muir was of the few, and she was not to be taken lightly. But her influence was neutralized by the solid immobility of her husband. He had never done anything sudden in his life. Every resolve was the result of a long process of thought, and every act of importance had to be previewed from all possible points. An honest man, strongly religious and a great admirer of Tom Skyler, he was slow-moving as a glacier, although with plenty of fire in him deep down.

"He's sound at the heart, my man Robbie," his wife said to Skyler, "but he's terrible deliberate. Wait a bit,

109

laddie. He'll come around."

"But meantime the summer's going and nothing will be done," was Skyler's impatient answer.

So a meeting was called to discuss the question of building a church, with the result that the five men and three women present decided that for the present nothing could be done. This was really Robbie Muir's opinion, though he refused to do or say anything but grunt, as Skyler told to me afterwards. It is true, Williams the storekeeper just come from "across the line," did all the talking, but no one paid much attention to his fluent fatuities except as they represented the unexpressed mind of the dour, exasperating Scotchman Muir, who sat silent but for an "ay" now and then, so expressive and conclusive that everyone knew what he meant, and that discussion was at an end. The schoolhouse was quite sufficient for the present; the people were too few and too poor and they were getting on well under the leadership of their present minister. These were the arguments which Robbie's "ay" stamped as quite unanswerable.

It was a sore blow to Skyler, who had set his heart upon a church, and neither Mrs. Muir's "hoots" at her husband's slowness nor her promises that she "would make him hear it" could relieve his gloom.

In this state of mind he rode up with me to pay our weekly visit to the little girl shut up in her lonely house among the hills.

It had become Skyler's custom during these weeks to turn for cheer to that little room, and seldom was he disappointed. She was so bright, so brave, so cheery, and so full of fun, that gloom faded from her presence as mist before the sun.

Gwen's bright face—it was almost always bright now—and her bright welcome did something for The Pilot. But the feeling of failure was upon him. Not that he confessed either to failure or gloom; he was far too true a man for that. But Gwen felt his depression in spite of all his brave attempts at brightness, and insisted that he was ill. She asked me what was wrong.

"Oh, it's only his church," I said, proceeding to give her an account of Robbie Muir's silent, solid inertness, and how he had blocked the minister's scheme.

"What a shame!" cried Gwen, indignantly, "What a bad man he must be!"

Skyler smiled. "No, indeed," he answered, "why, he's the best man in the place, but I wish he would say or do something. If he would only get mad and swear I think I should feel happier."

Gwen looked quite mystified.

"You see, he sits there in solemn silence looking so tremendously wise that most men feel foolish if they speak, while as for doing anything, the idea appears preposterous in the face of his immovableness."

"I can't bear him!" cried Gwen. "I should like to stick pins in him."

"I wish someone would!" answered Skyler with a laugh. "It would make him seem more human if he could be made to jump."

"Try again," said Gwen, "and get someone to make him jump."

"It would be easier to build the church," said Skyler.

"I could make him jump," said Gwen, "and I *will*," she added after a pause.

"You!" answered Skyler, opening his eyes. "How?"

"I'll find some way," she replied resolutely.

And so she did.

For when the next meeting was called to consult about the building of a church, the congregation—usually made up chiefly of farmers and their wives with Williams the storekeeper—was greatly surprised to see Bronco Bill, Hi, and half a dozen ranchers and cowboys walk in at intervals and solemnly seat themselves.

111

Robbie looked at them with surprise and a little suspicion. In church matters he had no dealings with the Samaritans from the hills, and while, in their unregenerate condition, they might be regarded as suitable objects of missionary effort, as to their having any part in the direction of the church policy—from such a notion Robbie was delivered by his loyal adherence to the scriptural injunction that he should not cast pearls before swine.

Skyler, though surprised to see Bill and the cattlemen, was none the less delighted, and faced the meeting with more confidence. He stated the question for discussion: Should a church building be erected this summer in Swan Creek? And he put his case well. He showed the need of a church for the sake of the men in the district, the families growing up, the incoming settlers, and for the sake of the country and its future. He called upon all who loved their church and their country to unite in this effort. It was an enthusiastic appeal and all the women and some of the men were at once upon his side.

Then followed dead, solemn silence. Robbie was content to wait till the effect of the speech should be dissipated in smaller talk. Then he gravely said:

"The kirk wad be a gran' thing, nae doot, an' they wad all dootless"—with a suspicious glance toward Bill —"rejoice in its erection. But we must be cautious, an' I wad like to enquire hoo much money a kirk cud be built for, and whaur the money wad come frae?"

Skyler was ready with his answer. The cost would be $1,200. The Church Building Fund would contribute $200, the people could give $300 in labor, and the remaining $700, he thought, could be raised in the district in two years' time.

"Ay," said Robbie, and the tone and manner were sufficient to drench any enthusiasm with the chilliest of water.

So much was this the case that the chairman, Williams, seemed quite justified in saying, "it is quite evident that the opinion of the meeting is adverse to any attempt to load the community with a debt of one thousand dollars," and he proceeded with a very complete statement of the many and various objections to any attempt at building a church this year. The people were very few, they were dispersed over a large area, they were not sufficiently interested, they were all spending money and making little in return; he supposed, therefore, that the meeting might adjourn.

Robbie sat silent and expressionless in spite of his little wife's anxious whispers and nudges, when the meeting was unexpectedly interrupted by Bill.

"Say, boys!" he said, "they ain't much behind this project of their's, heh?" The low, drawling voice was perfectly distinct and arresting.

"Seems they ain't got no use for a new church," was the answer from one of his friends in the dark corner.

"Old Scotchie takes his religion out in prayin', I guess," drawled Bill, "but wants to sponge for a place t' do it in."

This reference to Muir's proposal to continue using the school moved the youngsters present to giggling, and made the Scotchman squirm, for he prided himself on his ability to pay his way.

"A blanked lot o' psalm-singing freeloaders!"

"Order! Order!" cried the chairman.

By now Muir was in a most uncomfortable state. So unusually stirred was he that for the first time in memory he made a motion.

"I move we adjourn, Mr. Chairman," he said in a voice vibrating with emotion.

"Tryin' to end the meeting on us, eh, boys?" drawled Bill.

"But the meetin' ain't out yet," replied Hi.

"Ye can bide till mornin'," said Robbie angrily, beginning to put on his coat, "I'm gaen home."

Hi sprang to the door, and stood there waiting in delighted expectation for his friend's lead. Robbie looked at him, then at his wife, and hesitated. Then Bill stood up and began to speak.

"Mr. Chairman, I have a few remarks—"

"Go on!" yelled his friends from the dark corner of the room. "Hear! Hear!"

"I know this ain't hardly my game. This here Sky Pilot's not too proud t' invite a feller on Sunday afternoons. But them that runs the shop don't seem to want us fellers round too much."

Robbie was staring intently at Bill, and at this shook his head, muttering angrily, "Hoots! Nonsense! Ye're welcome enough!"

"But," Bill went on slowly, "I guess I been on the wrong track. I been of the opinion that these fellers," pointing to Muir, "was stuck on religion, which I ain't much myself, and really were concerned about the blocking o' the devil, which The Pilot says can't be done without a regular Gospel factory. O' course it ain't no business of mine, but if us fellers was really set on anything for the good o' our Order"—(Bill was a brotherhood man)—"I b'lieve I know where five hundred dollars maybe could perhaps be got."

"You bet!...Hear! Hear!" yelled a chorus of approval.

"O' course, I ain't no bettin' man," Bill went on, "as a regular thing, but I'd gamble a few jist here on this point. If the boys was stuck on anythin' costin' about seven hundred dollars, it seems likely t' me they'd git it in about two days."

Here Robbie grunted out an "ay" of such contemptuous unbelief that Bill paused, and looking over Robbie's head, he drawled out, even more slowly and mildly:

"I ain't much given t' bettin', as I said before, but if a man shakes money at me on that proposition, I'd accommodate him—"

"Hear! Hear!" yelled Hi again from the door.

"—Not bein' too bold, I believe that even for this here Gospel plant, seein' that the Pilot's rather set on it, I believe the boys could find five hundred dollars inside a month, if perhaps these religious fellers here could wiggle the rest out of their pants."

By now Robbie was good and angry and, stung by the taunting, he broke out suddenly, "Ye'll not be able t' make that guid, I dinna doobt."

"Do you mean I ain't prepared t' back it up?"

"Ay," replied Robbie.

"Ain't likely I'll be called on to. I guess my five hundred is safe enough," drawled Bill, drawing him on.

"Ow ay!" he said, "the two hunner will be here from us, an' will nae doobt wait lang eneuch fer yer share."

"I ain't got no paper on my person," said Bill, "but if some gentleman would mark down the date, I'll lay my name on it that in one month from today there will be five hundred dollars on that there desk lookin' round for two hundred more maybe, or perhaps you would incline to two fifty," he drawled in his most winning tone to Robbie, who was growing more impatient every moment.

"No matter t' me. Ye're ravin' like a daft loon anyway."

"You will make a record o' this little transaction, boys, and perhaps the schoolmaster will write it down," said Bill.

It was all carefully taken down, and amid much enthusiastic confusion the ranchers and their gang carried Bill off to Old Latour's, while Robbie Muir, in deep wrath but in dour silence, went off through the dark with his little wife following several steps behind him. His chief grievance, however, was against the chairman for "allooin' sich a disorderly pack o' loons t' disturb respectable fowk," for he could not hide the fact that he had been made to break through his accustomed defense of immovable silence.

The sorest point with poor Robbie was not only that Bill had cast doubt upon his religious sincerity, which the little man could not endure, he had also held him up to the ridicule of the community, which was painful to his pride. But when he understood, some days later, that Bill was taking steps to back up his offer and had been heard to declare that "he'd make them pious ducks take water if he had to put up a year's pay," Robbie went quietly to work to make good his part of the bargain. For his Scotch pride would not allow him to refuse a challenge from such a quarter.

15.
BILL'S PARTNER

The next day everyone was talking of Bill's bluffing the church people, and there was much quiet chuckling over Robbie Muir's discomfort.

Tom Skyler was equally distressed and bewildered, for Bill's conduct, so very unusual, had only one explanation—the usual one for any folly in that country: drunkenness.

"I wish he had waited till after the meeting to go to Latour's. He spoiled the last chance I had," he said sadly.

"But he may have accomplished something," I suggested.

"He was only giving Muir 'a song and dance,' as he would say. The whole thing, I'm sure, means nothing."

But when I told Gwen the story of the night's proceedings, she was delighted with Bill's grave speech and his success in drawing out the canny Scotchman.

"Oh, lovely! Dear old Bill. Isn't he just lovely? Now he'll do something."

"Who, Bill?"

"No, that Scottie." This was her name for the immovable Muir.

"Not he, I'm afraid. Bill was just bluffing him. But it was good sport."

"I knew he'd do something."

"Who? Scottie?" I asked, for her pronouns were perplexing.

"No!" she cried, "Bill! He promised he would, you know," she added.

"So you were at the bottom of it?" I said.

"Oh, dear!" she kept laughing. "Dear old Bill."

Before I left that day from giving Gwen her lessons, Bill himself came to the Old Timer's ranch, inquiring in a casual way "if the 'boss' was in."

"Oh, Bill!" called out Gwen, "Come in here at once; I want you."

After some delay and some shuffling with hat and spurs, Bill lounged in and sat his lanky form upon the extreme end of a bench at the door, trying to look unconcerned as he remarked, "Gittin' cold. Shouldn't wonder if we'd have a little snow."

"Oh, come here," cried Gwen impatiently, holding out her hand. "Come here and shake hands."

Bill hesitated, then rose and swayed awkwardly across the room toward the bed. He took Gwen's hand and shook it up and down, then hurriedly said:

"Fine day, ma'am; hope I see you quite well."

"No, you don't," cried Gwen, laughing immoderately, but keeping hold of Bill's hand, to his great confusion she added, "I'm not well a bit. But I'm a great deal better since hearing of your meeting, Bill."

To this Bill made no reply, being entirely engrossed in getting his hard, bony, brown hand out of the grasp of the white, clinging fingers.

"Oh, Bill," went on Gwen. "How did you do it?"

But Bill, who had by this time got back to his seat at

the door, pretended ignorance of any achievement. He "hadn't done nothin' more out of the way than usual."

"Oh, don't talk nonsense!" cried Gwen, impatiently. "Tell me how you got Scottie to lay you two hundred and fifty dollars."

"Oh, that!" said Bill, in great surprise, "That ain't nuthin' much."

"But how did you get Scottie?" persisted Gwen. "Tell me, Bill," she added, in her most coaxing voice.

"Well," said Bill, "it was easy as rollin' off a log. I made the remark as how the boys generally put up for what they wanted without no fuss, and that if they was set on havin' a Gospel building I thought maybe they'd put up for it, the seven hundred dollars, and even as it was, seein' as The Pilot appeared to be set on to it, if them fellers would find two hundred and fifty, we could get the rest."

He paused, looking at Gwen's laughing face.

"Go on, Bill" she said, wiping away her tears and subduing her laughter.

"There ain't no more," said Bill. "He bit, and the schoolmaster here put it down."

"Yes, it's here sure enough," I said, "but I don't suppose you mean to follow it up, do you?"

"You don't, eh? Well, I am not responsible for your supposin', but them that is familiar with Bronco Bill generally expects him to back up his undertakin's."

"But how in the world can you get five hundred dollars from the cowboys for a church?"

"I hain't done the arithmetic yet, but it's safe enough. You see, it ain't the church altogether, it's the reputation of the boys."

"I'll help, Bill," said Gwen.

Bill nodded his head slowly and said, "Proud to have you," trying hard to look enthusiastic.

"You don't think I can," said Gwen.

Bill protested against such an imputation. "But I

can." Gwen went on. "I'll get daddy and The Duke too. And I'll give all my money. But it isn't very much," she added, sadly.

"Much?" said Bill, "if the rest of the fellows play up to that lead there won't be any trouble about that five hundred."

Gwen was silent for some time, then said with an air of resolve—

"I'll give my pinto!"

"Nonsense!" I exclaimed, while Bill declared "there warn't no call for such a thing."

"Yes. I'll give the pinto!" said Gwen decidedly. "I'll not need him any more," her lips quivered. "And besides, I want to give something I like. And Bill will sell him for me!"

"Well," said Bill, slowly, "it might be pretty hard to sell that there pinto."

Gwen began to exclaim indignantly, and Bill hurried on to say, "Not but what he ain't a good little horse for his weight, good little horse, but for cattle—"

Why, Bill, there isn't a better cattle horse anywhere!"

"Yes, that's so," assented Bill. "That's so, if you've got the rider. But put one of them rangers on him and it wouldn't be no fair show. You see," he explained, "he ain't a horse you could yank round and slam into a bunch of steers."

Gwen shuddered. "Oh, I wouldn't think of selling him to any of those cowboys." Bill crossed his legs and hitched round uncomfortably on his bench. "I mean one of these rough men that don't know how to treat a horse." Bill nodded, looking relieved. "I thought that someone like you, Bill, who knew how to handle a horse —"

Gwen paused, then added, "I'll ask The Duke."

"No call for that," said Bill hastily, "not but what The Duke ain't all right as a judge of a horse. But The

Duke ain't got the connection, it ain't his line." Bill hesitated. "But, if you are real set on to sellin' that pinto, come to think I guess I could find a sale for him, though, of course, I think perhaps that figure won't be high."

So it was finally arranged that the pinto should be sold and that Bill should see to the selling of it.

It was characteristic of Gwen that she would not say farewell to the pony on whose back she had spent so many hours of freedom and delight. When once she gave him up, she refused to allow her heart to cling to him anymore.

It was characteristic, too, of Bill that he led off the pinto after night had fallen, so that "his pardner" might be saved the pain of the parting.

"This here's rather a new game for me, but when my pardner," here he jerked his head towards Gwen's window, "calls for trumps, I'm blanked if I don't throw my highest, if it costs a leg."

16.
BILL'S FINANCING

Bill's method of conducting the sale of the pinto was eminently successful as a financial operation, but there are those in the Swan Creek country who have never been able to understand the mystery attached to the affair. It was at the fall roundup, which this year ended at the Ashley Ranch. There were representatives from all the ranches and some cattlemen from across the border. The hospitality of the Ashley Ranch was up to its own high standards, and after supper the men were in a state of high exhilaration. The Honorable Fred and his wife Lady Charlotte acted as hosts for the day with heartiness and grace.

After supper the men gathered round the big fire piled up before the long low shed, which stood open in front. It was such a wild and picturesque scene as can only be witnessed in the western ranching country. Around the fire, most of them wearing "chaps" and all of them with wide, hard-brimmed cowboy hats, the men grouped themselves, some reclining upon skins thrown upon the ground, some standing, some sitting, smoking, laughing, chatting, all in highest spirits and humor.

They had just finished their season of work. Their minds were full of long, hard rides, wild and varying experiences with mad cattle and bucking broncos and anxious watchings through hot nights, when a breath of wind or a coyote's howl might set the herd off in a frantic stampede, wolf hunts and badger fights and all the adventures that fill up a cowboy's summer. But tonight they were free men and of independent means, for their season's pay was in their pockets. The day's excitement, too, was still in their blood, and they were ready for anything.

Bill, as king of the bronco-busters, moved about with the slow, careless indifference of a man confident of his position and sure of his ability to maintain it.

He spoke seldom and slowly, was not as quick witted as his partner, Hi Kendall, but in action he was swift and sure, and "in trouble" he could be counted on.

"Hello, Bill," said a friend, "where's Hi? Ain't seen him around!"

"Well, don't just know. He was going to bring up my pinto."

"Your pinto? Whar'd ye git him? Good for cattle?"

The crowd began to gather.

Bill grew mysterious, and even more than usually reserved.

"Good, fer cattle! Well, I ain't much on gamblin' but I've got a few dollars that says that there pinto can outwork any bronco in this outfit, givin' him a fair show after the cattle."

The men became interested.

"Where was he raised?"

"Dunno."

"Where'd ye get him?" Across the border?"

"No," said Bill stoutly, "right in this country. The Duke there knows him."

123

This at once raised the pinto several points. To be known, and as Bill's tone indicated, favorably known by The Duke, was a testimonial to which any horse might aspire.

"Where'd ye get him, Bill? Don't be so blanked uncommunicatin'!" said an impatient voice.

Bill hesitated. Then, with an apparent burst of confidence, he assumed his frankest manner and voice.

"Well," he said, taking a fresh chew and offering a plug to his neighbor, who passed it on after helping himself, "ye see, it was like this. Ye know that little Meredith girl?"

Chorus of answers, "Yes! The red-headed one. I know! She's a reg'lar blizzard!"

Bill paused, stiffened himself a little, dropped his frank air and drawled out in cool, hard tones, "I might remark that that young lady is, I might presume to say, a friend of mine."

In the pause that followed murmurs were heard extolling Gwen's many excellences, and Bill yielded to the requests for the continuation of his story. As he described her and her pinto and her work on the ranch, the men, many of whom had had glimpses of her, gave emphatic approval in their own way. But as he told of her rescue of Joe and of the sudden tragedy that had come upon her, a great stillness fell upon the crowd and the men listened with their eyes shining in the firelight with growing intentness. Then Bill spoke of The Sky Pilot and how he stood by her and helped her and cheered her; "and now," concluded Bill, "when The Pilot is in a jam she wants to help him out."

"Right enough," said one. "How's she going to work it?" said another.

"Well, he's dead set on buildin' a church, and them fellas down at the Creek that does the prayin' and such don't seem to back him up!"

"What's the hitch, Bill?"

"Oh, they don't want to dig into their own pockets and pay for it."

"How much?"

"Why, he only asked 'em for seven hundred and would give 'em two years, but they bucked—wouldn't look at it."

"What did you do, Bill?"

"Oh," said Bill, modestly, "I didn't do much. Gave 'em a little bluff."

"What?"

But Bill remained silent, till under strong pressure, and as if making a clean breast of everything, he said:

"Well, I just told 'em that if you boys made such a fuss about anythin' like they did about their Gospel outfit, an' I ain't sayin' against it, you'd put up seven hundred without turnin' a hair."

"That's the stuff! What did they say to that, eh, Bill?"

"Well," said Bill, slowly, "they *called* me!"

"That so? And what did you do, Bill?"

"Gave 'em a dead straight bluff!"

"Did they take you on, Bill?"

"Well, I reckon they did. The schoolmaster here put it down."

At that, I read the terms of the agreement.

There was a chorus of hearty approvals of Bill's course in "not letting them talk their way out of it."

Then slowly the responsibility of the situation began to dawn upon them, when someone asked:

"How are you going about it, Bill?"

"Well," drawled Bill, with a touch of sarcasm in his voice, "there's that pinto."

"Pinto be blanked!" said young Bill, "Say, boys, is that little girl going to lose that one pony of hers to help out her friend, The Pilot? Good fellow, too, he is!"

A chorus followed of, "Not by a long sight;...we'll put up the stuff!"

"Then," went on Bill, even more slowly, "there's The Pilot, he's going to ante up a month's pay of his own. He might make it two," he added thoughtfully.

But Bill's proposal was scorned with groans. "Twenty-eight a month ain't much for a man to save money out of to educate himself," Bill continued, as if thinking aloud. "Of course he's got his mother at home, but she can't make much more than her own livin', though she might help him some."

This was altogether too much for the crowd. By now they had consigned Bill and his plans to failure.

"Of course," Bill explained, "if that's how you boys feel about it. Maybe I was bein' a little swift in givin' 'em the bluff."

"No, you wasn't! We'll see you out! There's between twenty and thirty of us here."

"I should be glad to contribute thirty or forty if need be," said The Duke, who was standing not far off, "to assist in the building of a church. It would be a good thing, and I think the parson should be encouraged. He's the right sort."

"I'll cover your thirty," said another, and so it went from one to another in tens and fifteens and twenties, till within half an hour I had entered three hundred and fifty dollars in my book, with Ashley yet to be heard from, which meant fifty more. It was Bill's hour of triumph.

"Boys," he said, with solemn emphasis, "ye're all right. But the little pale-faced girl, that's what I'm thinkin' on. Won't she open them big eyes of hers! I know this'll tickle her."

The men were greatly pleased with Bill and even more pleased with themselves. Bill's picture of the "little girl" and her tragic lot had gone to their hearts and, with men of that breed, it was one of their few luxuries to yield to their generous impulses. Most of them had few opportunities to lavish love and sympathy upon worthy objects and, when the opportunity came, all that was best in them clamored for expression.

17.
HOW THE PINTO SOLD

The glow of virtuous feeling following their generous actions prepared the men for a keener enjoyment than usual of a night's sport. They had just begun to settle themselves in groups about the fire for poker and other games when Hi rode up into the light and with him a stranger on Gwen's beautiful pinto pony.

Hi was evidently half drunk and, as he swung himself off his bronco, he saluted the company with a wave of the hand.

Bill, looking curiously at Hi, went up to the pinto and, taking him by the head, led him up into the light, saying:

"See here, boys, here's that pinto of mine I was telling you about."

"Hold on there!" said the stranger, "this here horse belongs to me, if paid-down money means anything in this country."

"The country's all right," said Bill in an ominously quiet voice, "but this here pinto's another transaction I reckon."

128

"The horse is mine, I tell you," said the stranger in a loud voice.

The men began to crowd around with faces growing hard. It was dangerous in that country to play fast and loose with horses.

"Look here mates," said the stranger with a Yankee drawl. "I ain't no horse thief, and if I ain't bought this horse and paid down good money then it ain't mine—if I have, it is. That's fair, ain't it?"

At this Hi pulled himself together, and in a half-drunken tone declared that the stranger was right, and then he handed a roll of money to Bill.

"You get off that pony," said Bill to the stranger, "till this thing is settled."

There was something so terrible in Bill's manner that the man contented himself with blustering and swearing, while Bill turned to Hi and said:

"Did you sell this pinto to him?"

Hi was able to acknowledge that, being offered a good price, and knowing that his partner was always ready for a deal, he had sold the pinto to the stranger for forty dollars.

Bill groaned in agony.

"Ain't the horse, but the little girl," he said. But his partner's deal was as good as his own, and angry as he was he knew he could not attempt to break the bargain.

At this moment the Honorable Fred, noting the unusual excitement about the fire, approached, followed at a little distance by his wife and The Duke.

"Perhaps he'll sell," he suggested quickly to Bill.

"No," said Bill sullenly, "He's a mean cuss."

"I know him," said Ashley, "let me try him." He walked over to the stranger, but the man declared that the pinto suited him down to the ground and he wouldn't take twice his money for him.

In vain they haggled and bargained with him, but

the man was immovable. Eighty dollars he wouldn't look at, a hundred hardly made him hesitate. At this point Lady Charlotte came down into the light and stood by her husband, who explained the circumstances to her. She had already heard Bill's description of Gwen's accident and of her part in the church-building scheme. There was silence for a few moments as she stood looking at the beautiful pony.

"What a shame the poor child should have to part with the dear little creature!" she said in a low tone to her husband. Then, turning to the stranger, she said in a clear sweet tone, "What would you ask for him?"

He hesitated and then said, lifting his hat awkwardly, "I was just remarking how that pinto would fetch one hundred and fifty dollars down into Montana. But seein' as a lady is enquirin', I'll put him down to one hundred and twenty-five."

"Too much," she said promptly, "far too much, is it not, Bill?

"Well," drawled Bill, "if it were a feller as was used to ladies he'd offer you the pinto, but he's too mean even to come down to the even hundred."

The Yankee took him up quickly. "Well, if I were so durned—pardon, madam"—taking off his hat, "used to ladies as some folks would like to think themselves, I'd buy that there pinto and make a present of it to this here lady as stands before me."

Bill twisted uneasily.

"But I ain't goin' to be mean." The Yankee went on, "I'll give that pinto up for the even money for the lady if any man cares to put up the stuff."

"Well, my dear," said Ashley with a bow, "we cannot well let that dog lie."

She turned and smiled at him, and the pinto was transferred to the Ashley stables, to Bill's outspoken delight, who declared he "couldn't have faced the music if that there pinto had gone across the line."

I confess, however, I was somewhat surprised at the ease with which Hi escaped his wrath, and my surprise was in no way lessened when I saw, later in the evening, the two partners with the stranger taking a quiet drink out of the same bottle with evident mutual admiration and delight, and a long slow wink from Bill, which passed into a frown as he caught my eye. My suspicion was aroused that the sale of the pinto might bear investigation, and this suspicion was deepened when Gwen next week gave me a rapturous account of how wonderfully Bill had disposed of the pinto, showing me bills for one hundred-fifty dollars! To my look of amazement Gwen replied:

"You see, he must have got them bidding against each other, and besides, Bill says pintos are going up."

It all began to come clear to me, but I only answered that I knew they had risen very considerably in value within a month. The extra fifty was Bill's.

I was not present to witness the finishing of Bill's bluff, but was told that when Bill made his way through the crowded aisle and laid his five hundred and fifty dollars on the schoolhouse desk, the look of disgust, surprise and finally of pleasure on Robbie Muir's face, was worth a hundred more. But Robbie was ready and put down his two hundred with the single remark:

"Ay! Ye're no as daft as ye look," amid roars of laughter from all.

Then The Pilot, with eyes and face shining, rose and thanked them all. But when he told of how the little girl in her lonely shack in the hills thought so much of the church that she gave up her beloved pony for it, her one possession, the light from his eyes glowed in the eyes of all.

The men from the ranches who could best understand the full meaning of her sacrifice and who also could realize the full measure of her calamity, were stirred to their hearts' depths, so that when Bill remarked in a very distinct undertone, "I don't doubt that this here Gospel shop wouldn't be materializin' into its present shape but for that little girl," there rose noises of approval in a variety of tones that left no doubt that all present agreed with his opinion.

But though Skyler never could quite get at the complete truth of Bill's measures and methods, and was doubtless all the more uncomfortable in mind for that, he had no doubt that while Gwen's influence was the moving spring of action, Bill's bluff had a good deal to do with the "materializin' " of the first church in Swan Creek.

Whether Fred Ashley ever understood the peculiar style of Bill's financing, I do not quite know. But if he ever did come to know, he was far too much of a man to make a fuss. Besides, I fancy the smile on his lady's face was worth a great deal to him. At least, so the look of proud and fond love in his eyes seemed to say as he turned away with her from the fire the night of the pinto's sale.

18.
THE LADY CHARLOTTE

The night of the pinto's sale was a momentous night to Gwen, for then it was that the Lady Charlotte's interest in her began. Momentous, also, to the Lady Charlotte. For it was that night which brought The Sky Pilot into her life.

I had turned back to the fire around which the men had fallen into groups and was prepared to have an hour's delight, for the scene was full of wild beauty, when The Duke came and touched me on the shoulder.

"Lady Charlotte would like to see you."

"Why?"

"She wants to hear about this affair of Bill's."

We went through the kitchen into the large dining room, at one end of which stood a stone chimney and fireplace. Lady Charlotte had said that she did not much care what kind of house the Honorable Fred would build for her, but that she must have a fireplace.

She was very beautiful—tall, slight, and graceful in

every way. There was a reserve and a grand air in her bearing that put people in awe of her. Yet as I entered the room she welcomed me with such kindly grace and I felt instantly at ease.

"Come and sit by me," she said, drawing an armchair into the circle about the fire. "I want you to tell us all about some things."

"You see what you're in for, Connor," said her husband. "It is a serious business when my lady takes one in hand."

"As he knows, to his own cost," she said, smiling and shaking her head at her husband.

"So I can testify," put in the Duke.

"Ah! I can't do anything with you," she replied, turning to him.

"I am your most abject slave," he replied with a profound bow.

"If you only were," she replied smiling at him—a little sadly, I thought—"I'd keep you out of all sorts of mischief."

"Quite true, Duke," said her husband, "just look at me."

"Come!" broke in Lady Charlotte. "You are turning my mind away from my purpose."

"Is it possible, do you think?" said The Duke to her husband.

"Not in the very least," he replied, "if my experience counts for anything."

But Lady Charlotte turned her back upon them and said to me:

"Now, tell me first about Bill's encounter with the funny little Scotchman."

I then told her the story of Bill's bluff in the best style I could. She was greatly amused and interested.

"And Bill has really got his share of the money ready," she cried. "It is very clever of him."

"Yes," I replied, "but Bill is only the very humble

instrument, the moving spirit of the thing is another."

"Oh, yes, you mean the little girl that owns the pony," she said. "That's another thing you must tell me about."

"The Duke knows more than I do," I replied, "my acquaintance with her is only recent; his is lifelong."

"Why have you never told me of her?" she asked, turning to The Duke.

"Haven't I told you of the little Meredith girl? Surely I have," said Duke, hesitating.

"Now, you know quite well you have not, and that means you are deeply interested. Oh, I know you well," she said.

"He is the most secretive man," she went on to me, "shamefully and ungratefully reserved."

The Duke smiled, then said, "Why she's just a child. Why should you be interested in her? No one was," he added sadly, "till misfortune brought her to everyone's attention."

Her eyes grew soft, and her gay manner changed. Then she said to The Duke gently, "Tell me about her now."

It was evidently an effort, but he began his story of Gwen from the time he saw her first, years ago, playing in and out of her father's rambling shack, shy and wild as a young fox. As he went on with his tale, his voice dropped into a low musical tone, and he seemed as one dreaming aloud. Unconsciously he put into the tale much of himself, revealing how great an influence the little child had had upon him, and how empty of love his life had been in this lonely land. Lady Charlotte listened with her face intent upon him, and even her quiet husband was conscious that something more than usual was happening. He had never heard The Duke break through his proud reserve before.

When The Duke told the story of Gwen's awful fall,

which he did with great descriptiveness, a little red spot burned upon the Lady Charlotte's pale cheek, and as The Duke finished this tale with the words, "It was her last ride," she covered her face with her hands and cried:

"Oh, Duke, it is horrible to think of! But what splendid courage!"

"Great stuff! eh, Duke?" cried Ashley, kicking a burning log vigorously.

But The Duke made no reply.

"How is she now, Duke?" said Lady Charlotte.

The Duke looked up as from a dream. "Bright as the morning," he said. Then in reply to Lady Charlotte's look of wonder, he added, "The Pilot did it. Connor will tell you. I don't understand it myself."

"Tell me," said Lady Charlotte very gently.

Then I told her how, one by one, we had failed to help her, and how Skyler had ridden up that morning through the canyon, and how he had brought the first light and peace to her by his marvelous pictures of the flowers and ferns and trees and all the wonderful mysteries of that wonderful canyon.

"But that wasn't all," said The Duke quickly when I stopped.

"No," I said slowly, "that was *not* all by a long way. But the rest I don't understand. That's The Pilot's secret."

"Tell me what he did," said Lady Charlotte softly again. "I want to know."

"I don't think I can," I replied. "He simply read out of the Scriptures, and talked to her."

Lady Charlotte looked disappointed.

"Is that all?" she said.

"It is quite enough for Gwen," said The Duke confidently, "for there she lies, often suffering, always longing for the hills and the free air, but with her face radiant as the flowers of the beloved canyon."

136

"I must see her," said Lady Charlotte, "and that wonderful preacher."

"You'll be disappointed in him," said The Duke.

"Oh, I've seen him and heard him, but I don't know him," she replied. "There must be something in him that one does not observe at first."

"So I have discovered," said The Duke. And with that the subject was dropped, but not before Lady Charlotte made me promise to take her to Gwen, The Duke being strangely unwilling to do so.

"You'll be disappointed," he said. "She is only a simple little child."

But Lady Charlotte thought differently. And having made up her mind on the matter, there was nothing for it, as her husband said, but "for all hands to surrender and the sooner the better."

And so the Lady Charlotte had her way, which, as it turned out, was much the wisest and best.

19.
THROUGH GWEN'S WINDOW

When I told Skyler of Lady Charlotte's purpose to visit Gwen, he was not too well pleased.

"What does she want with Gwen?" he said. "She will just put notions into her head and make the child discontented.

"Why should she?" I asked.

"She won't mean to, but she belongs to another world. And Gwen cannot talk to her without getting glimpses of a life that will make her long for what she can never have," replied Skyler.

"But suppose it is not idle curiosity in Lady Charlotte," I suggested.

"I don't say it is quite that," he answered, "but these people love a sensation."

"I don't think you know Lady Charlotte," I replied. "I hardly think from her tone the other night that she is a sensation hunter."

"At any rate," he answered decidedly, "she is not to worry poor Gwen."

I was a little surprised at his attitude, and felt that

he was unfair to Lady Charlotte. But I didn't argue with him on the matter. He could not bear to think of any person or thing threatening Gwen's peace.

The very first Saturday after my promise was given, we were surprised to see Lady Charlotte ride up to the door of our shack early in the morning.

"You see, I am not going to let you off," she said as I greeted her. "And the day is so very fine for a ride."

I apologized for not taking her to Gwen sooner, and then to get out of my difficulty, rather meanly turned toward Skyler, and said:

"The Pilot doesn't approve of our visit."

"And why not, may I ask?" said Lady Charlotte, lifting her eyebrows.

Skyler's face burned, partly with vexation at me, and partly with embarrassment for Lady Charlotte had put on her grand air. But he stood to his guns.

"I was saying, Lady Charlotte," he said, looking straight into her eyes, "that you and Gwen have little in common—and—and—" he hesitated.

"Little in common!" said Lady Charlotte quietly. "She has suffered greatly."

The Pilot was quick to catch the note of sadness in her voice.

"Yes," he said, wondering at her tone, "she has suffered greatly."

"And," continued Lady Charlotte, "she is bright as the morning, Duke says." There was a look of pain in her face.

The Pilot's face lit up. He came nearer and laid his hand caressingly upon her beautiful horse.

"Yes, thank God!" he said quickly, "bright as the morning."

"How can that be?" she asked, looking down into his face. "Perhaps she would tell me."

"Lady Charlotte," said the preacher with a sudden flush, "I must ask your pardon. I was wrong. I thought you—" he paused, "but go to Gwen, she will tell you, and you will do her good."

"Thank you," said Lady Charlotte, putting out her hand, "and perhaps you will come and see me too."

Skyler promised to do so and stood looking after us as we rode up the trail.

"There is something more in your Sky Pilot than at first appears," she said. "The Duke was quite right."

"He is a great man," I said with enthusiasm, "tender as a woman and with the heart of a hero."

"You and Bill and The Duke seem to agree about him," she said, smiling.

Then I told her tales of The Pilot, and of his ways with the men, till her blue eyes grew bright and her beautiful face lost its proud look.

"It is perfectly amazing," I said, finishing my story, "how these devil-may-care rough fellows respect him, and come to him in all sorts of trouble. I can't understand it. He is just a boy."

"No, not amazing," said Lady Charlotte slowly. "I think I understand it. He has a true man's heart, and holds a great purpose in it. I've seen men like that. Not clergymen I mean, but men with a great purpose."

Then, after a moment's thought, she added:

"But you ought to care for him better. He does not look strong."

"Strong!" I exclaimed quickly. "He can do as much riding as any of us."

"Still," she replied, "there's something in his face that would make his mother anxious."

In spite of my repudiating her suggestion, I found myself for the next few minutes thinking of how he would become exhausted and faint from his long rides. I resolved that he must have a rest and change.

It was one of those early September days, the best of all in the western country, when the light falls less fiercely through a soft haze that seems to fill the air about you, and then grows into purple on the far hill-tops. By the time we reached the canyon the sun was riding high and pouring its rays full into all the deep nooks where mostly shadows lay.

There were no shadows today, except such as the trees cast upon the green moss beds and the black rocks. The tops of the tall elms were rusty, but the leaves of the rugged oaks that fringed the canyon's lips shone a rich and glossy brown. All down the sides the poplars and delicate birches, pale yellow but some-times flushing into orange and red, stood shimmering in the golden light. Here and there the broad-spread-ing, feathery sumacs made great splashes of brilliant crimson upon the yellow and gold. Down in the bottom stood the cedars and the balsams, still green. We stood some moments silently gazing into this tangle of inter-lacing boughs and shimmering leaves, all glowing in yellow light. Then Lady Charlotte broke the silence in tones soft and reverent as if she stood in a great ca-thedral.

"And this is Gwen's canyon!"

"Yes, but she never sees it now," I said, for I could never ride through without thinking of the child to whose heart this was so dear, but whose eyes never rested upon it. Lady Charlotte made no reply. We took the trail that wound down into this maze of mingling colors and lights and shadows. Everywhere lay the fal-len leaves, brown and yellow and gold—everywhere on our trail, on the green mosses and among the dead ferns. As we rode, leaves fluttered down from the trees above silently through the tangled boughs and lay with the others on moss and rock and beaten trail.

The flowers were all gone, but the Little Swan sang as ever its many-voiced song, as it flowed in pools and eddies and cascades, with here and there a golden leaf upon its black water. Ah! How often in weary, dusty days these sights and sounds and silences have come back to me and brought my heart rest!

As we began to climb up into the open, I glanced at my companion's face. The canyon had done its work with her as with all who loved it. The touch of pride that was the habit of her face was gone. In its place rested the earnest wonder of a little child, while in her eyes lay the canyon's tender glow. And with this face we arrived and she looked in upon Gwen.

Gwen, who had been waiting for her, immediately forgot all her nervous fear. With hands outstretched she cried out in welcome:

"Oh, I'm so glad! You've seen it and I know you love it! My canyon, you know!" she went on, answering Lady Charlotte's mystified look.

"Yes, dear child," said Lady Charlotte, bending over the pale face with its halo of golden hair. "I love it." But she could get no further. Her eyes were full of tears. Gwen gazed up into the beautiful face, wondering at her silence, then said gently:

"Tell me how it looks today! The Pilot always shows it to me. Do you know," she added thoughtfully, "The Pilot looks like it himself. He makes me think of it, and—and—" she went on shyly, "you do too."

By this time Lady Charlotte was kneeling by the couch, smoothing the beautiful hair and gently touching the face so pale and lined with pain.

"That is a great honor, truly," she said brightly through her tears—"to be like your canyon, and like your Pilot."

Gwen nodded, but she was not to be denied.

"Tell me how it looks today," she said. "I want to see it. Oh, I want to see it!"

Lady Charlotte was greatly moved by the yearning in the voice, but controlling herself, she said gaily, "I can't show it to you as Thomas Skyler can, but I'll tell you what I saw."

"Turn me where I can see," said Gwen to me.

I faced her bed toward the window and raised her up so that she could look down the trail toward the canyon's mouth.

"Now," she said, after the pain of the lifting had passed, "tell me, please."

Then Lady Charlotte set the canyon before her in rich and radiant coloring, while Gwen listened, gazing down upon the trail to where the elm tops could be seen.

"Oh, it is lovely!" said Gwen, "and I see it so well. It is all there before me in my mind when I look through my window."

Lady Charlotte looked at her, wondering at her bright smile. At last she could not help the question:

"But don't you long to see it with your own eyes?"

"Yes," said Gwen gently. "Often I want it, oh, so much!"

"Then, Gwen dear, how do you bear it?" Her voice was eager and earnest. "Tell me, Gwen. I have heard all about your canyon flowers, but I can't understand how the fretting and pain went away."

Gwen looked at her, first in amazement, then in dawning understanding.

"Have you a canyon, too?" she asked gravely.

Lady Charlotte paused a moment, then nodded. It did appear strange to me that she should break down her proud reserve and open her heart to this child.

"And there are no flowers, Gwen, not one," she said rather bitterly, "nor sun nor seeds nor soil, I fear."

"Oh, if only The Pilot were here, he would tell you."

At this point, feeling that they would rather be alone, I excused myself on the pretext of looking after the horses.

What they talked of during the next hour I never knew, but when I returned to the room Lady Charlotte was reading slowly and with perplexed face to Gwen

143

out of her mother's Bible the words "for the suffering of death, crowned with glory and honor."

"You see even for Him, there was suffering," Gwen said eagerly. "But I can't explain it all. The Pilot will make it clear." Then the talk ended.

We had lunch with Gwen—bannocks and fresh sweet milk and blueberries—and after another hour of gay fun we came away.

Lady Charlotte kissed her tenderly as she bade Gwen good-by.

"You must let me come again and sit at your window," she said, smiling down upon the wan face.

"I shall watch for you. How good that will be!" cried Gwen with delight. "How many come to see me! You make five." Then she added softly, "You will write your letter."

But Lady Charlotte shook her head.

"I can't do that, I fear," she said, "but I shall think of it."

It was a bright face that looked out upon us through the open window as we rode down the trail. Just before we took the dip into the canyon, I turned to wave my hand.

"Gwen's friends always wave from here," I said, wheeling my bronco around.

Again and again Lady Charlotte waved her handkerchief.

"How beautiful, but how wonderful!" she said as if to herself. "Truly, *her* canyon is full of flowers."

"It is quite beyond me," I answered. "The preacher may explain it."

"Is there anything your Sky Pilot can't do?" said Lady Charlotte.

"Try him," I ventured.

"I mean to," she replied. "But I fear I cannot bring anyone to my canyon," she added in an uncertain voice.

As I left her at her door, she thanked me with courteous grace.

"You have done a great deal for me," she said, giving me her hand. "It has been a beautiful, wonderful day."

When I told Skyler all the day's doings, he burst out:

"What a stupid and self-righteous fool I have been! I never thought there could be any canyon in her life. How short our sight is!" All the rest of that night I could get almost no words from him.

That was the first of many visits to Gwen. Not a week passed but Lady Charlotte took the trail to the Meredith ranch and spent an hour at Gwen's window. Often Skyler found her there. But though they were always pleasant hours to him, he would come home in great anxiety about Lady Charlotte.

"She is perfectly charming and doing Gwen no end of good, but she is proud as an archangel. She has had an awful break with her family at home and with no family here, no child that is, it is eating away at her and spoiling her life. She told me so much, but she will allow no one to touch the affair."

One day we met her riding toward the village. As we drew near, she drew up her horse and held up a letter.

"Home!" she said. "I wrote it today, and I must get it off immediately."

Skyler understood her at once, but he only replied:

"Good!" but with such emphasis that we both laughed.

"Yes, I hope so," she said with the red beginning to show in her cheek. "I have dropped some seed into my canyon."

"I think I see the flowers beginning to sprout already," said The Pilot.

She shook her head doubtfully and replied:

145

"I shall ride up and sit with Gwen at her window."

"Do," replied The Pilot, "the light is good there. Wonderful things are to be seen through Gwen's window."

"Yes," said Lady Charlotte softly. "Dear Gwen!—but I fear it is often made bright with tears."

As she spoke she wheeled her horse and cantered off, for her own tears were not far away.

I followed her in thought up the trail winding through the round-topped hills and down through the golden lights of the canyon and into Gwen's room. I could see the pale face, with its golden aureole, light up and glow as they sat before the window, while Lady Charlotte would tell her how Gwen's Canyon looked today and how in her own bleak canyon there were the first signs of flowers to come.

20.

THE BUILDING OF THE CHURCH

The building of the Swan Creek Church made a sensation in the country. And all the more that Bronco Bill was in command.

"When I put in my money I stay with the game," he announced. And stay he did, to the great benefit of the work and to the delight of The Pilot, who was wearing his life out in trying to do several men's work.

It was Bill who organized the crews to haul stone for the foundation and logs for the walls. It was Bill who assigned the various jobs to those volunteering service. To Robbie Muir and two stalwart Glengarry men from the Ottawa lumber region, who knew all about the broadaxe, he gave the hewing down of the logs that formed the walls. When they were done, Bill declared they were "better'n a sawmill." It was Bill too who carried out the financing. His business with Williams, the storekeeper from "the other side" who dealt in lumber and building material, was such as to establish forever Bill's reputation in finance.

With Skyler's plans in his hands, Bill went to Williams, finding a time when the store was full of men after their mail.

"What do you think of them plans?" he asked innocently.

Williams was full of opinions and criticism and suggestions, all of which were gratefully, even humbly received.

"Kind of hard to figger out jest how much lumber'll go into the shack," said Bill, "ye see the logs makes a difference."

To Williams the thing was simplicity itself, and after some figuring, he handed Bill a complete statement of the amount of lumber of all kinds that would be required.

"Now what would that there come to?"

Williams named his figure. Then Bill entered upon negotiations.

"I ain't no man to beat down prices. No, sir, I say give a man his figger. Of course, this here ain't my doing. Besides, bein' a Gospel shop the price naterally would be different, right?"

To this the boys standing around all assented. Williams looked uncomfortable.

"In fact"—and Bill adopted his public tone, to Hi's admiration—"this here's a public institution for the good of the community."

"That's so! Right you are!" chorused the boys gravely.

Williams agreed, but declared he had thought of all this in making his calculation. But seeing it was a church, and the first church and their own church, he would make a cut in the price, which he did after more figuring. Bill gravely took the slip of paper and put it into his pocket without a word. By the end of the week, having in the meantime ridden into town and interviewed the dealers there, Bill sauntered into the store and took up his position across the floor from Williams.

"You'll be wanting that sheeting, won't you, next week, Bill?" said Williams.

"What sheetin's that?"

"Why, for the church. Ain't the logs up?"

"Yes, that's so. I was just goin' to see the boys here about gettin' it hauled," said Bill.

"Hauled!" said Williams in amazed indignation. "Ain't you goin' to stick to your deal?"

"I generally make it my custom to stick to my deals," said Bill, looking straight at Williams.

"Well, what about your deal with me last Monday night?" said Williams angrily.

"Let's see. Last Monday night," said Bill, apparently thinking back, "can't say as I remember any particular deal. Any of you fellers remember?"

No one could recall any deal.

"You don't remember getting any paper from me, I suppose?" said Williams, sarcastically.

"Paper! Why, I believe I've got that there paper on me at this very moment," said Bill diving into his pocket and drawing out Williams' estimate. He spent a few moments in careful scrutiny.

"There ain't no deal on this as I can see," said Bill, gravely passing the paper to the boys, who each scrutinized it and passed it on with a shake of the head or a remark as to the absence of any sign of a deal.

Then Williams changed his tone. For his part, he was indifferent in the matter.

So Bill made him an offer.

"Of course, I believe in supportin' local folks' industries, and if you can touch my figure I'd be glad to give you the contract."

Bill's figure, which was quite fifty percent lower than Williams' best offer, was rejected as quite impossible.

"Thought I'd make you the offer," said Bill casually, "seein' as the boys here'll all be doing buildin' of their own in the future and will likely go where they can get the best deal, I believe in standin' up for local trades and manufactures, but we gotta go elsewhere if the price be lower."

There were nods of approval on all sides, and Williams was forced to accept for the sake of the future of his business. Bill began arranging with the Hill brothers and Hi to make an early start on Monday. It was a great triumph.

Second in command in the church building enterprise stood Lady Charlotte. Under her labored her husband, The Duke, and indeed all the company of the Noble Seven. Her home became the center of a new type of social life. With great tact, and much was needed for this kind of work, she drew the bachelors from their lonely shacks and from their wild carousals, and gave them a taste of the joys of a pure home-life, the first they had had since leaving the old homes years ago. Then she made them work for the church with such zeal and diligence that Ashley and Duke declared that ranching had become quite an incidental interest since the church-building had begun. The Pilot went about with a radiant look on his pale face, while Bill gave it forth as his opinion, "though she was a little high in the action, she could hit an uncommon gait."

Bill pushed the work of construction with such energy that by the first of December the church stood roofed, sheeted, floored and ready for windows, doors and ceiling. Skyler began to hope that he would see the desire of his heart fulfilled—the church of Swan Creek open for services on Christmas Day.

During these weeks there was more than church-building going on, for while the days were given to the shaping of logs and the driving of nails and the planing of boards, the long winter evenings were spent in talk around the fire in my shack. There for some months past The Pilot had made his home and Bill, since the beginning of the church building, had come "to camp." Those were memorable nights for The Pilot and Bill, and indeed for me too, and the other boys who, after a day's work on the church, were often brought in by Bill or Skyler.

Great nights they were for us all. After bacon and beans and bannocks, and occasionally potatoes or a pudding, with rich and steaming coffee to wash all down, pipes would follow, and then yarns of adventures—possible and impossible—all exciting and wonderful, and all received with the greatest credulity.

If, however, the powers of belief were put to too great a strain by a tale of more than ordinary marvel, Bill would follow with one of such utter impossibility that the company would feel that the limit had been reached, and the yarns would cease. But after the first week, most of the time was given to Skyler, who would read to us of the deeds of the mighty men of old who had made and wrecked empires.

What happy nights they were to those cowboys who had been cast up like driftwood upon this strange and lonely shore! Some of them had never known what it was to have a thought beyond the work and sport of the day. And the world into which Skyler was ushering them was all new and wonderful.

21.
HOW BILL HIT THE TRAIL

When the crowd remained with us, Skyler read us all sorts of tales of adventures in all lands by heroes of all ages. But when we three sat together by our fire, The Pilot would always read us tales of the heroes of sacred story. And these delighted Bill more than those of any of the ancient empires of the past. He had his favorites. Abraham, Moses, Joshua, and Gideon never failed to arouse his admiration. But Jacob was to him always "a mean cuss," and David he could not appreciate. Most of all he admired Moses and the Apostle Paul, whom he called "that little chap." But when the reading was about the One Great Man that shone majestic amid the gospel stories, Bill made no comments; He was too high for approval.

By and by Bill began to tell these tales to the boys himself, and one night, when a quiet mood had fallen upon the company, Bill broke the silence.

"Say, Pilot, where was it that the little chap got mixed up in that riot?"

"Riot?" said Skyler.

"Yes. You remember when he stood off the whole gang from the stairs?"

"Oh yes, at Jerusalem!"

"Yes, that's the spot. Perhaps you would read that to the boys. Good yarn! Little chap, you know, stood up and told 'em they were all sorts of blanked thieves and cut-throats, and stood 'em off. Played it alone too."

Most of the boys failed to recognize the story in its new dress. There was much interest.

"Who was the duck? Who was the gang? What was the row about?"

"The Pilot here'll tell you," Bill replied. Then to Skyler he added, "If you'd kind o' give 'em a lead before you begin, they'd catch on to the yarn better."

"Well, it was at Jerusalem," began The Pilot, when Bill interrupted, "If I might remark, perhaps it might help the boys onto the trail maybe, if you'd tell 'em how the little chap struck his new gait." So he designated the Apostle's conversion.

Then Skyler introduced the Apostle with some formality to the company, describing with such vivid touches his life and early training, his sudden wrench from all he held dear under the stress of a new conviction, his magnificent enthusiasm and courage, his tenderness and patience, that I was surprised to find myself regarding him as a sort of hero, and the boys were all ready to back him against any odds. As Skyler read the story of the arrest at Jerusalem, stopping now and then to picture the scene, we saw it all and were in the thick of it. The raging crowd hustling and beating the life out of the brave little man, the sudden thrust of the disciplined Roman guard through the mass, the rescue, the pause on the stairway, the calm face of the little hero beckoning for a hearing, the quieting of the frantic, frothing mob, the fearless speech—all passed before us.

The boys were thrilled.

"Good stuff, eh?"

"Yeah," drawled Bill, highly appreciating their marks of approval. "That's what I call a partickler fine character of a man."

"You bet!" said Hi.

"I say," broke in one of the boys who was just emerging from the tenderfoot stage, "o' course that's in the Bible, ain't it?"

The Pilot assented.

"Well, how do you know it's true?"

The Preacher was proceeding to elaborate his argument when Bill cut in somewhat more abruptly than usual.

"Look here, young feller!" Bill's voice was in the tone of command. "How do you know anything's true? How do you know The Pilot here's true when he speaks? Can't you tell by the feel? You know by the sound of his voice, don't you?"

Bill paused and the young fellow agreed readily.

"Well, how do you know a durned son of a she jackass when you see him?"

Again Bill paused. There was no reply.

"Well," said Bill, resuming his deliberate drawl. "I'll give you the information without extra charge. It's by the sound he makes when he opens his blanked jaw."

"But," went on the young skeptic, nettled at the laugh that went round, "that don't prove anything. You know," turning to Skyler, "there are heaps of people who don't believe the Bible."

The Pilot nodded.

"Some of the smartest, best-educated men are agnostics," proceeded the young man, warming to his theme and failing to notice the stiffening of Bill's lank figure. "I don't know but what I am one myself."

"That so?" said Bill with sudden interest.

"I guess so," was the modest reply.

"Got it bad?" went on Bill, with a note of anxiety in his tone.

But the young man turned to Skyler and tried to open a fresh argument.

"Whatever he's got," said Bill to the others in a mild voice, "it's spoilin' his manners. Seems as if he ought to take somethin'," said Bill, in a voice suspiciously mild. "What would you suggest?"

"A walk maybe!" said Hi.

"I hold the opinion that you have mentioned an uncommonly vallable remedy, better'n Pain Killer."

Bill rose slowly.

"I say," he drawled, tapping the young fellow, "it appears to me a little walk would perhaps be good."

"All right, wait till I get my cap," was the unsuspecting reply.

"I don't think you will need it. I think you'll be warm enough." Bill's voice had unconsciously passed into a sterner tone. Hi was on his feet and at the door.

"This here interview is private *and* confidential," said Bill to his partner.

"Exactly," said Hi, opening the door. At this the young fellow, who was a strapping six-footer but soft and flabby, drew back and refused to go.

He was too late. Bill's grip was on his collar and out they went into the snow. Behind them Hi closed the door. In vain the young fellow struggled to wrench himself free from the hands that had him by the shoulder and the back of the neck. I took it all in from the window. He might have been a boy for all the effect his plungings had upon the long, sinewy arms that gripped him so fiercely. After a minute's furious struggle the young fellow stood quiet, then Bill suddenly shifted his grip from the shoulder to the seat of his buckskin trousers. Then began a series of movements before the house—up and down, forward and back, which the unfortunate victim, with hands wildly clutching at empty air, was quite powerless to resist till he was brought up panting and gasping and subdued to a standstill.

"I'll learn you several other kinds of tricks," said Bill, his drawl lengthening perceptibly. "Come round here, will you, and shove your blanked second-handed trash down our throats?" Bill paused to get words, then burst out again:

"I've a notion to—"

"Don't! Don't! For Heaven's sake!" cried the struggling man. "I'll stop it! I will!"

Bill at once lowered him and set him on his feet.

"All right! Shake!" he said, holding out his hand, which the other took with caution.

It was a remarkably sudden conversion and lasting in its effect. There was no more agnosticism in the little group that gathered around The Pilot for the nightly reading.

The interest in the reading kept growing night by night. Skyler was accomplishing his work, especially with Bill, though Bill did not know it. I remember one night when the others had gone, The Pilot was reading to us the Parable of the Talents, Bill was particularly interested in the servant who failed in his duty.

"Ornery cuss, eh?" he remarked. "Served him blamed well right, in my opinion!"

But when the practical bearing of the parable became clear to him, after a long silence, he said slowly:

"Well, that there seems to indicate that it's about time for me to get a rustle on."

Then, after another silence, he said with hesitation, "This here church-buildin' business now, do you think that'll perhaps count? Ain't much, o' course, anyway."

Poor Bill, he was like a child. The Pilot handled him with a mother's touch.

"What are you best at, Bill?"

"Bronco-bustin' and cattle," said Bill, wondering what bearing that had on the parable of the talents, "that's my line."

"Well, Bill, my line is preaching just now, and 'piloting' you know." The preacher's smile was like a sunbeam on a rainy day. There were tears in his eyes and voice. "And we have just got to be faithful to what He gives us to do. You see what He says, 'Well done, good and *faithful* servant. Thou hast been *faithful*.'"

Bill was puzzled.

"Faithful!" he repeated. "Does that mean with the cattle, perhaps?"

"Yes, that's just it, Bill, and with everything else that comes your way."

Bill never forgot that lesson, for I heard him with a kind of quiet enthusiasm giving it to Hi as a great find. "Now I call that a fair deal," he said to his friend, "gives every man a show. No cards up the sleeve."

"That's so," was Hi's thoughtful reply, "distributes the trumps among everyone."

Somehow Bill gradually came to be regarded as an authority on questions of spirituality and morals. No one ever accused him of "gettin' religion." He went about his work in his slow quiet way, but he was always sharing his discoveries with "the boys." If anyone puzzled him with subtleties he never rested till he had him face to face with The Pilot.

So it came that these two drew to each other with more than brotherly affection. When Bill got into difficulty with problems that have vexed the souls of men far wiser than he, Skyler would either disentangle the knots or would turn his mind to the truths that stood out sure and clear, and Bill would be content.

"That's good enough for me," he would say, and his heart would be at rest.

22.
THE OPENING OF THE
SWAN CREEK CHURCH

When, near the end of the year, The Pilot fell sick with an influenza, Bill nursed him like a mother and sent him off for a rest and change to Gwen, forbidding him to return till the church was finished. Bill himself rode up to visit him twice a week. The love between the two was most beautiful, and when I find my heart growing hard from time to time, and unbelieving in men and things, I let my mind wander back to a scene that I came upon one night in front of Gwen's house. These two were standing alone in the clear moonlight, Bill with his hand upon The Pilot's shoulder, and The Pilot with his arm around Bill's neck.

"Dear old Bill," The Preacher was saying, "dear old Bill," and the voice was breaking into a sob.

And Bill, standing stiff and straight, looked up at the stars, coughed and swallowed hard for some moments, then said in a queer croaky voice:

"Shouldn't wonder if a chinook would blow up."

"Chinook?" laughed The Pilot with a catch in his voice. "You dear old humbug," and he stood watching till the lank form swayed down into the canyon.

The day of the church opening came, as all days, however long waited for, will come—a bright beautiful Christmas Day. The air was still and full of frosty light, as if arrested by a voice of command, waiting the word to move. The hills lay asleep under their dazzling coverlet. Back of all, the great peaks lifted majestic heads out of the dark forests and gazed with calm steadfast faces upon the white sunlit world. Today, as the light filled up the cracks that wrinkled their hard faces, they seemed to smile, as if the Christmas joy had somehow moved something in their old stony hearts.

The people were all there—farmers, ranchers, cowboys, wives, and children—all happy, all proud of their new church, and now all expectant, waiting for the Sky Pilot and the Old Timer, who were to drive down if Skyler was fit and were to bring Gwen if the day was fine. As the time passed on, Bill, as master of ceremonies, began to grow uneasy.

Then Indian Joe appeared and handed a note to Bill. He read it, grew gray in the face and passed it to me. Looking, I saw in poor, wavering lines the words, "Dear Bill. Go on with the opening. Sing the Psalm, you know the one, and say a prayer. And oh, come to me quick, Bill. Your Pilot."

Bill gradually pulled himself together, announced in a strange voice, "Our Pilot can't come," handed me the Psalm, and said:

"Make them sing."

It was that grand Psalm for all hill peoples, "I to the hills will lift mine eyes," and with wondering faces they sang the strong, steadying words. After the Psalm was over the people sat and waited. Bill looked at the Honorable Fred Ashley, then at Robbie Muir, then said to me in a low voice:

"Kin you make a prayer?"

I shook my head, ashamed as I did so of my cowardice.

Again Bill paused, then said:

"The Pilot says there's got to be a prayer. Can anyone make one?"

Again dead, solemn silence.

Then Hi, who was near the back, came to his partner's help, "What's the matter with you trying yourself, Bill?"

The red began to come up in Bill's white face.

"Ain't in my line. But The Pilot says there's got to be a prayer, and I'm going to stay with the game."

Then leaning on the pulpit, he said:

"Let's pray," and began:

"God Almighty, I ain't no good at this, and perhaps you'll understand if I don't put things right." Then a pause followed, during which I heard some of the women beginning to sob.

"What I want to say," Bill went on, "is we're mighty glad about this church, which we know it's you and The Pilot that's worked it. And we're all glad to chip in."

Then again he paused, and looking up, I saw his hard, gray face working and two tears stealing down his cheeks. Then he started again:

"But about The Pilot—I don't want to presume—but if you don't mind, we'd like to have him stay—in fact, don't see how we kin do without him—look at all the boys here. He's just getting his work in and is bringin' 'em right along, and God Almighty, if You take him away it might be a good thing for himself, but for us—oh, God..."

The voice quivered and was silent. "Amen."

Then someone, I think it must have been the Lady Charlotte, began, "Our Father, Who art in heaven..." and all joined that could join to the end.

For a few moments Bill stood up, looking at them silently. Then as if remembering his duty, he said, "This here church is open. Excuse me."

He stood at the door, gave a word of direction to Hi, who had followed him out. Then he left on his bronco and shook him out into a hard gallop.

The Swan Creek Church was opened. The form of service may not have been correct, but if great love counts for anything and praying faith, then all that was necessary was done.

23.
THE DAY OF THE COWBOYS' GRIEF

In the old times a funeral was regarded in the Swan Creek country as a kind of solemn festivity. In those days, for the most part, men died in their boots and were planted with much honor and loyal celebration. There was often neither shroud nor coffin, and in the Far West many a poor fellow lies as he fell, wrapped in his own or his comrade's blanket.

But when we gathered at the Meredith ranch to carry The Pilot out to his grave, it was felt that the Foothill Country was called to a new experience. They were all there. The men from the Porcupine and from beyond the Fort, the Mounted Police with the Inspector in command, all the farmers for twenty miles around, and of course all the ranchers and cowboys of the Swan Creek country.

There was no effort at repression. There was no need. For in the cowboys, for the first time in their experience, there was no heart for fun. As they rode up and hitched their horses to the fence or drove their sleighs into the yard and took off the bells, there was no loud-voiced salutation, but with silent nod they took their places in the crowd about the door or passed into the kitchen.

The men from the Porcupine could not quite understand the gloomy silence. It was something unprecedented in a country where men laughed all care to scorn and saluted death with a nod. But they were quick to read signs, and with characteristic courtesy they fell in with the mood they could not understand. There is no man living so quick to feel your mood, and so ready to adapt himself to it, as is the true Westerner.

This was the day of the cowboys' grief. To the rest of the community The Sky Pilot was preacher; to them he was comrade and friend. They had been slow to admit him to their confidence. But steadily he had won his place with them, till within the last few months they had come to count him as of themselves.

He had ridden the range with them; he had slept in their shacks and cooked his meals on their tin stoves; and besides, he was Bill's chum. That alone was enough to give him a right to all they owned. He was theirs, and they were only beginning to take full pride in him when he passed out from them, leaving an emptiness in their life new and unexplained. No man in that country had ever shown concern for them, nor had it occurred to them that any man could, till green Thomas Skyler came. It took them long to believe that the interest he showed in them was genuine and not simply professional. Then, too, from a preacher they had expected chiefly pity, warning, rebuke.

Skyler astonished them by giving them respect, admiration, and open-hearted affection. It was months before they could get over their suspicion that he was humbugging them. When once they did, they gave him back without knowing it all the trust and love of their big generous hearts. He had made this world new to some of them, and to all had given glimpses of the next. It was no wonder that they stood in silent groups about the house where the man who had done all this for them and had been all this to them, now lay dead.

There was no demonstration of grief. The Duke was in command, and his quiet, firm voice, giving directions, helped all to self-control. The women who were gathered in the middle room were weeping quietly. Bill was nowhere to be seen, but near the inner door sat Gwen in her chair with Lady Charlotte beside her holding her hand. Her face, worn with long suffering, was pale, but serene as the morning sky and with not a trace of tears. As my eye caught hers, she beckoned me to her.

"Where's Bill?" she said. "Bring him in."

I found him at the back of the house.

"Aren't you coming in, Bill?" I said.

"No. I guess there's plenty without me," he said in his slow way.

"You'd better come in. The service is going to begin," I urged.

"Don't seem as if I cared for to hear anythin' much. I ain't much used to preachin' anyway," said Bill with careful indifference. But he added to himself, "except his of course."

"Come in, Bill," I urged. "It will look funny, you know, without you."

But Bill replied, "I guess I'll not bother."

I reported to Gwen, who answered in her old urgent way, "Tell him I want him."

I took the message to Bill.

"Why didn't you say so before?" he said. Starting up, he walked into the house and took up his position behind Gwen's chair. Opposite and leaning against the door stood The Duke with a look of quiet earnestness on his handsome face. At his side stood the Honorable

164

Fred Ashley, and behind him the Old Timer, looking bewildered and grief-stricken. The Pilot had filled a large place in the old man's life. The rest of the men stood about the room and filled the kitchen beyond, all quiet, solemn, sad.

In Gwen's room, the one farthest in, lay The Pilot— stately and beautiful under the magic touch of death. As I stood and looked down upon the quiet face I saw why Gwen shed no tear but carried instead a look of serene triumph. She had read the face aright. The lines of weariness that had been growing so painfully clear the last few months were smoothed out, the look of care was gone, and in place of weariness was the proud smile of victory and peace. He had met his foe and was surprised to find his terror gone.

The service was beautiful in its simplicity. The minister, The Pilot's chief, had come out from town to take charge. He was rather a little man, but sturdy and well set. His face was burnt and seared with the suns and frosts he had braved for years. Still in the prime of his manhood, his hair and beard were grizzled and his face deep-lined, for the toils and cares of a pioneer missionary's life are neither few nor light. But out of his kindly blue eyes looked the heart of a hero, and as he spoke to us we felt the prophet's touch and caught a gleam of the prophet's fire.

"I have fought the fight," he read. The ring in his voice lifted up all our heads, and as he pictured to us the life of that battered hero who had written these words, I saw Bill's eyes begin to gleam and his lank figure straighten out its lazy angles. Then he turned the leaves quickly and read again, "Let not your heart be troubled...in my father's house are many mansions."

His voice took a lower, sweeter tone. He looked over our heads and for a few moments spoke of the eternal hope. Then he came back to us, and looking round into the faces turned so eagerly to him, talked to us of Thomas Skyler—how at the first he had sent him to us with fear and trembling—he was so young—but how he had come to trust in him and to rejoice in his work, and to hope much from his life. Now it was all over. But he felt sure his young friend had not given his life in vain.

He paused as he looked from one to the other, till his eyes rested on Gwen's face. I was startled, as I believe he was too, at the smile that parted her lips, so evidently saying, "Yes, but how much better I know than you."

"Yes," he went on after a pause, answering her smile, "you all know better than I that his work among you will not pass away with his removal, but will endure while you live." The smile on Gwen's face grew brighter. "And now you must not grudge him his reward and his rest...and his home."

Bill, nodding his head slowly, said under his breath, "That's so."

Then they sang that hymn of the dawning glory of Immanuel's land—Lady Charlotte playing the organ and The Duke leading with clear, steady voice, verse after verse. When they came to the last stanza the minister made a sign and, while they waited, he read the words:

"*I've wrestled on towards heaven*
'Gainst storm, and wind, and tide."

And so on to the last victorious cry,—

"*I hail the glory dawning*
In Immanuel's Land."

For a moment it looked as if the singing could not go on, for tears were on the minister's face and the women were beginning to sob, but The Duke's clear, quiet voice caught up the song and steadied them all to the end.

After the prayer they all went in and looked at Skyler's face and passed out, leaving behind only those that knew him best. The Duke and the Honorable Fred stood looking down upon the quiet face.

"The country has lost a good man, Duke," said Ashley. The Duke bowed silently. Then Lady Charlotte came and gazed a moment.

"Dear Pilot," she whispered, her tears falling fast. "Dear, dear Pilot! Thank God for you! You have done much for me." Then she stooped and kissed him on his cold lips and his forehead.

Then Gwen seemed to suddenly waken as from a dream. She turned and, looking up in a frightened way, said to Bill hurriedly:

"I want to see him again. Carry me."

Bill gathered her up in his arms and took her in. As they looked down upon the face with its proud peace, touched with the stateliness of death, Gwen's fear passed away, but when Duke started to cover the face, Gwen drew a sharp breath and, clinging to Bill, said with a sudden gasp:

"Oh, Bill, I can't bear it alone. I'm afraid alone."

She was thinking of the long, weary days of pain before her that she must face now without The Pilot's touch and smile and voice describing her beloved, their beloved, canyon.

"I know," said Bill, thinking of the days before him.

Gwen looked in his face a moment, then said, "We'll help each other," and Bill swallowed hard. He could only nod his head in reply. Once more they looked upon The Sky Pilot, leaning down and lingering over him, and then Gwen said quietly:

"Take me away, Bill."

Bill carried her to the window where the sun was reappearing from behind a cloud. Turning back I caught a look on The Duke's face so full of grief that I could not help showing my amazement. He noticed and said:

"The best man I ever knew, Connor. He had done something for me too...I'd give the world to die like that."

Then he covered his face.

We sat at Gwen's window, Bill, with Gwen in his arms, and I, watching. Down the sloping, snow-covered hill wound the procession of sleighs and horsemen, without sound of voice or jingle of bell. One by one they passed out of our sight and dipped down into the canyon. But we knew every step of the winding trail and followed them in our minds through that fairy scene of mystic wonderland. We knew how the great elms and the poplars and the birches clinging to the snowy sides interlaced their bare boughs into a network of bewildering complexity, and how the cedars and balsams and spruces stood in the bottom, their dark boughs weighted down with heavy white mantles of snow, and how every stump and fallen log and rotting stick was made a thing of beauty by the snow that had fallen so gently on them in that quiet spot. And we could see the rocks of the canyon sides gleam out black from under overhanging snow-banks. And we could hear the song of the Swan in its many tones, now under an icy sheet, cooing comfortably, and then bursting out into sunlit laughter and leaping into a foaming pool, to glide away smoothly murmuring its delight to the white banks that curved to kiss the dark water as it fled. And where the flowers had been, the violets and the windflowers and the clematis and the columbine and all the ferns and flowering shrubs, there now lay the snow. Everywhere the snow, pure, white, and myriad-gemmed, but every flake a flower's shroud.

Out where the canyon opened to the sunny, sloping prairie, there they would lay The Pilot to sleep, within touch of the canyon he loved, with all its sleeping things.

And there he lies to this time.

Spring has come many times to the canyon since that winter day, and has called to the sleeping flowers, summoning them forth in merry troops, and ever more and more till the canyon ripples with them.

Lives are like flowers. In dying they abide not alone, but sow themselves and bloom again with each returning spring, and ever more and more.

Often during the following years, as here and there I came upon one of those that companied with us in those Foothill days, I would catch a glimpse, in word and deed and look, of him we called, first in jest but afterwards with true and tender feeling we were not ashamed to own, our Sky Pilot—young foothills preacher, Thomas Skyler.

Sunrise Books is committed to offering our readers quality, wholesome books. If you enjoyed this one, we hope you will try another Sunrise title.

Being in the bookstore business ourselves (Sunrise still operates out of the mail room and garage of our retail Christian bookstore), we always stress our hope that you will buy from your own local Christian bookstore. The bookstore ministry is a valuable one to every community and they need your support. However, if you do not have a store easily accessible to you, we at Sunrise are happy to send you our books. Below are listed Sunrise's titles currently available and some that are on the way.

SUNRISE BOOKS, PUBLISHERS CURRENT LIST OF TITLES (1988)

"Ann of the Prairie" Series

Vol. 1	**This Rough New Land**	by Kenneth Sollitt	ISBN 0-940652-03-X
Vol. 2	**Our Changing Lives**	by Kenneth Sollitt	ISBN 0-940652-04-8
Vol. 3	**These Years of Promise**	by Nick Harrison with Kenneth Sollitt	ISBN 0-940652-05-6

"Stories of Yesteryear" Series

Vol. 1	**Jim Craig's Battle for Black Rock**	by Ralph Connor	ISBN 0-940652-06-4
Vol. 2	**Thomas Skyler: Foothills Preacher**	by Ralph Connor	ISBN 0-940652-07-2
Vol. 3	**The Man From Glengarry**	by Ralph Connor	available 1989
Vol. 4	**The Prospector**	by Ralph Connor	available 1989
Vol. 5	**The Doctor**	by Ralph Connor	available 1990
Vol. 6	**Glengarry School Days**	by Ralph Connor	available 1990

The "Sunrise Centenary Editions" of the Works of George MacDonald

Leatherbound collectors editions of the original works of this bestselling 19th century Scottish author, available as a handsome uniform set for the first time in this century. Single copy prices of these heirloom editions, $27.50. Member subscription rates are available at a reduced rate. Printings are in an individually numbered, limited basis, so write for details and currently available titles in this expanding collection.

The Sunrise "Masterline" Series

Studies and essays about George MacDonald, his life, and his works by such leading MacDonald scholars and authorities as Rolland Hein, Michael Phillips, Richard Reis, and MacDonald's own sons. Write for details and a listing of titles in this growing series of important books.